EXPERIMENT IN MURDER

Moore dreams he's in the Lake District, climbing a mountain — carrying a woman's body — the woman he attacked as she slept in their hotel. He throws her body into the chasm at the summit and returns to the hotel. He wakes up. He examines his shoes: just as he left them before retiring, no trace of mud from the hillside . . . then it *has* all been a dream! But Moore, victim of an experiment in murder, finds his dream is real!

JOHN RUSSELL FEARN
Edited by Philip Harbottle

EXPERIMENT IN MURDER

Complete and Unabridged

LINFORD
Leicester

First published in Great Britain

First Linford Edition
published 2011

British Library CIP Data

Fearn, John Russell, *1908 – 1960.*
Experiment in murder. - -
(Linford mystery library)
1. Murderers- -England- -Lake District- -
Fiction. 2. Suspense fiction.
3. Large type books.
I. Title II. Series
823.9'12–dc22

ISBN 978–1–4448–0925–1

Published by
F. A. Thorpe (Publishing)
Anstey, Leicestershire

Set by Words & Graphics Ltd.
Anstey, Leicestershire
Printed and bound in Great Britain by
T. J. International Ltd., Padstow, Cornwall

This book is printed on acid-free paper

1

Experiment in Murder

I am a medium, and for reference purposes only I give my name as Henry Clifton, of London. As to the extent of my psychic abilities, I have little to say. Also, I must withdraw from all responsibility for the messages that came to me from John Carlow Moore after he had been executed. I only know that he chose me as the instrument through which to make the communication I have recorded here.

My name is John Carlow Moore. I first became acquainted with Enoch Pym in July of 1934. It happened in the casual manner common to potential vital happenings. I had taken a brief holiday in the Lakes, and there, at my little hotel near Coniston, reposed the man for whom I was destined to commit murder.

A curious fellow, Pym — short, inclined to be stout, with wild and disordered black hair surrounding a podgy, pasty face. This general facial outline, lent added insipidness by a big, pendulous mouth and pale but searching blue eyes, did little to make him prepossessing; and yet he held an uncanny fascination for me from the first moment I set eyes on him. Odd though it may sound, I am half inclined to think that it was his delightful voice that interested me. Nowhere had I ever heard so mellow an intonation, so smooth and flawless a diction.

He came into my life on my second day at the Lakes, when I returned from a happy, solo jaunt to Rydal to find him in the low, old-fashioned dining room of the hotel. He was seated at the spotless tea-table eating poached eggs on toast, surrounded by cakes, sugar, milk and teapot. He smiled at me pleasantly as I entered, and soon I was keeping him company with another poached egg. For a long time we were silent, mentally weighing each other up, as two Englishmen meeting for the first time in a lonely spot are wont to do; then at last he spoke, and that wonderful voice fell on my ears for the first time.

'My name is Pym — Enoch Pym,' he explained. 'Just up for a few days' fishing.'

I returned the introduction, told him of my efforts to escape hard work as a journalist for a week, and went on to elaborate on my inborn love for the Cumberland scenery. We talked far beyond the cakes and cigarettes, and continued as we took an evening stroll toward Coniston village. In a remarkably short space of time we had become the best of friends, which in itself is peculiar, for I had the journalist's intuition for detecting suspicious characters. Certainly, I never felt in Pym's presence that there was somewhere in his makeup a streak of incarnate cruelty.

Upon that glorious evening, he was civility itself. He revealed an amazing knowledge of all the subjects I touched upon in our conversation, from the printing of newspapers to affairs of the occult. And all the time his superb voice lulled me into a curious submission;

3

it droned on and on, merging flawlessly into the perfect calm of that summer eve. To our left lay Coniston Water; to the right, the gaunt and stern escarpments of Coniston Old Man, backed by the sullen ramparts of Dow Crags; and farther to the north, its grim needle-pointed spires piercing the misty gray of the paling sky, stood Helvellyn. Altogether it was a tranquilly ideal environment for two men with apparently kindred interests, and I think it was this isolation that caused me to listen with credence to Pym's observations on the subjects of mysticism, hypnotism, and the supernatural. Most certainly, I would never have listened with half as much seriousness in my native London.

'Suppose,' he said suddenly, jabbing a well-gnawed pipe in the air, 'that you were to die. Do you think you could find the way back? To here?'

I shook my head. 'I don't think I could. Mind you, I believe in afterlife but only as a closed book — another plane with which mortals of this plane cannot communicate.'

He seemed to ponder over that. We walked on again in silence for a space, smoking and pursuing our own thoughts; then he suddenly resumed.

'Frankly, Moore, I came up to the Lakes here to make an experiment. One might call it an experiment in hypnotism. I was expecting to secure the services of a farmer or labourer for my purposes, but since a good Providence has placed me in contact with you I feel that perhaps you might — '

'Why, surcly!' I exclaimed. 'If I can be of any service I shall be only too pleased. After all, two men in a lonely spot, like this . . . well, any diversion is welcome. What exactly are you going to do?'

'I don't quite know yet.'

He stopped in mid-stride and cast a glance at the darkening sky. 'It's getting dark, Moore,' he remarked, as though the topic of hypnotism had never been mentioned. 'We had better be getting back.'

★   ★   ★

That, I say, was how I met Pym. I have tried to convey my first reactions to his peculiar nature. He seemed, as I was with him day after day, to be pursuing some strange chimera of his own which controlled him with relentless power. Although he was always civil and pleasing, I had no doubts whatever about the moments of calm in which I often surprised him. While I was out walking with him this odd facet of his nature was completely absent. He would talk in that fascinating, half-husky voice of his and throw out quite meaningless comments about his intended experiment — but within the staid and almost gloomy walls of our little hotel he would relapse again.

More often than not I found him gazing through the window at the stern bulk of Coniston Old Man, shifting his gaze only to take in the view of the sullen ramparts of Dow Crags to the left of the mountain. It was as though they held for him an intangible magnetism, as though they stimulated within him some unsuspected mental foible. And once I caught him muttering half aloud, quite unaware of my presence in the low-ceilinged room.

' . . . it is a fate which I shall administer justly, not with my own hands, but with all the resources of my brain. There can be no other way.'

Strange observation indeed! I was looking at him curiously when he became abruptly aware of my presence. With a curious smile he joined me at the tea table and, with characteristic calmness, made no reference to his strange behaviour.

'My wife is joining me tonight,' he said, in a matter-of-fact voice, pouring out tea. This was a surprise to me; I had not even suspected he was married.

'I'm glad for your sake, Pym, but I shall miss our little walks,' I smiled. 'Really, I've enjoyed them.'

He gazed at me with those pale blue eyes. The strong summer evening light streaming through the end window of the room bathed one half of his peculiar, podgy face in intense radiance and threw the eyes into relief; they stared at me like glass circles, limpid blue rings with an intensely dark spot of pupil in their centres. Just for an instant they chilled me, stirred something strongly in my brain. In those moments it seemed as though the entire soul of Enoch Pym was laid bare before me. Here, I knew, was a man to be wary of; yet his wonderful voice gripped me in its inexplicable spell again as he began to speak.

'I really see no reason why our walks should be interfered with,' he remarked calmly, his eyes still upon me. 'I too have enjoyed them. The quiet mountain scenery, our mutual sociability — these are things to be treasured, Moore. As to my wife, she is a strange woman: moody, usually lost in introspections. I fancy she is only joining me because she enjoys mountain air. Certainly it is not my company she is seeking.'

'No, no — I see.' I nodded quickly, and rather than pry into the mysteries of his domestic life, I let the matter drop. For a time silence persisted between us, but I could feel his eyes upon me; then back came the superb diction to smooth my puzzled reflections.

'You will not like my wife, Moore.'

'No?' I looked up to meet his eyes.

'Why do you say that? I get on with most people.'

'Maybe, but you won't with my wife. You see, you will meet as enemies; you will not like her — your dislike will grow, too. Do you understand that, Moore? You will hate her — hate her!'

'I — I shall hate her,' I agreed slowly, trying to tear my eyes away from the bright glitter of the tea-things, the reflections from the silver teapot, the glare from the reflecting mirror on the wall; above all, away from those two pale blue pools in the expressionless face . . . If only I could break the spell of that perfect voice of his! Its tones sank into every fibre of my being; and for a time, how long I do not know, I was in a world that shimmered and danced with bright sun-lights, in a world mastered and controlled by a voice that assured me I would hate the woman Betty Pym. Finally, I knew I would hate her, but for heaven's sake do not ask me why!

'Marmalade?' he asked suddenly, and I shot out of my vague, indeterminate realm of cloudy thoughts and speculations to find him holding the silver-edged receptacle almost under my nose. Again the reflected sunlight beat from it into my eyes, so that I blinked,

'Sorry,' I said with an apologetic laugh, taking it from him. 'I — I was day dreaming, I think. You said something about your wife, I believe?'

'Did I?' He shrugged slightly; the man was an absolute chameleon of character — he veered perpetually from one thing to another, leaving me the more mystified every time. 'Perhaps I did,' he agreed doubtfully, lighting a cigarette. 'We don't get on very well, Betty and I . . . However, never mind, It won't interfere with our walks,'

And as though to substantiate it, we went out again after tea. It was that evening he went to endless trouble to point out to me the particular advantages and defects of Coniston Old Man and Dow Crags. I remember that we walked in the clear, sweet wind to the base of the mountain and there sat down upon a massive boulder. Pym had a heavy ebony walking stick with him, and with this he began to point out to my interested gaze certain landmarks with which he was manifestly familiar.

'You will notice, Moore, that at the extreme left of the mountain summit there is a chasm, all of seven hundred feet in depth, practically sheer, while opposite stand Dow Crags?'

I nodded, Shading my eyes from the glaring sun. His voice went on.

'The Dow Crags are available only to trained climbers, but anybody can climb the Old Man himself. Up the chasm between the two there blows a perpetual wind; it is not uncommon for climbers to slip and be carried away by it. And a body falling from either the Crags or the Old Man into that chasm is bound to be destroyed.'

'I see,' I answered, and although I have a reasonably good memory I never retained information with such vivid clarity before. It seemed as though the things he had told me had been driven into my brain with sledgehammer force; I soaked them in, pondered them, re-iterated them to myself all through the remainder of our evening ramble.

He talked on all kinds of topics afterward, but I cannot remember one of them.

My whole mind was obsessed by the knowledge of a chasm and the fact that I hated his wife! Curious? Yes, perhaps it was. There was I, a perfectly sane journalist, up for a fishing holiday, completely in the toils of this enigmatic man with the glorious voice and magnetic eyes. Try though I would, I could not shake off the impress of his personality. It held me body and soul.

When we got back to the hotel, his wife had arrived. My first impression of her as she sat in the tiny dining room, clearly illuminated in the specially generated electric light, was quite a favourable one. I completely forgot, for the time being, my ridiculous resolve to hate her. She was a small, dark woman with a pale, aristocratic face and oddly frightened brown eyes. From her appearance, I could better have imagined her as Pym's daughter than his wife. Clearly, he was considerably older.

He introduced us with that calm way he had, taking instant and masterful possession of the situation. She, for her part, remained strangely quiet, eating supper in silence and replying only in monosyllables to her husband's inquiries, as to her journey from home and reactions to the Lake District. It required little effort on my part to apprehend that there was a strong estrangement between them, though what it was I was too discreet to ask. I wondered, too, whether Pym had really told me I would hate her or whether I had imagined it. Certainly I could find nothing in her to dislike. She was interesting, but nothing more. The domination of Pym completely overshadowed her,

Finally, sensing how strained matters were, I went up to bed — and not half an hour later dropped into a doze . . .

The instant I dropped asleep, it seemed, I became prey to terrible and Satanic nightmares. All the events of the day rose up before me in a solid conglomeration, intensely magnified and potent, in the midst of which I struggled like a lost soul. There was Pym with his beautiful voice — Pym, receding, advancing, receding in perpetual reiteration; all face, now nothing but two unblinking eyes of pale and heartless blue illumined by a strong light Once again the flash and glitter of silvered tea-things smote upon my tortured vision.

'You will hate my wife, Moore! You will hate my wife, Moore! You will hate my — ' On and on, endlessly — a crazy, raging diapason of chanting words merged into the lunacy of the whole horrible nightmare. Then, presently, Pym's face seemed to blur, but still I heard his voice ringing loud and clear in the now disordered emptiness of my mind.

'A body falling into that chasm is bound to be destroyed . . . '
The voice receded, but the dream was as vivid as ever. I was staggering desperately, half-clothed, up the ragged side of Coniston Old Man! About me, in the chilling wind — for I seemed to be nearly at the summit of the mountain — stood moonlit desolation of boulders and stones. Far below, a reflected silver

streak, lay Coniston Water. Something was weighing me down tremendously. To my surprise I discovered that it was a body — a woman's body! Apparently I had carried her all the way up the mountainside.

Now the dream took on a vaguely rational aspect; an ordered sequence came from the midst of the ridiculous chaos. Only intermittently, now, did the divine voice of Pym call strongly above the moaning wind.

'You'll hate my wife, Moore! You'll hate my wife! A body falling into that chasm is bound to be destroyed!'

'Yes, yes!' I yelled back hoarsely. 'It's bound to be destroyed!'

'You'll hate my wife, Moore . . .'

I looked down again at the woman I had been carrying. She lived, but was quite unconscious, a deep wound on her forehead from which blood flowed slowly. Suddenly I realized that she was Pym's wife, and that I had stunned her and brought her here. Athwart my subconscious mind lay the recollection of how I had risen from my bed, dressed, and crept into the little Gothic bedroom where she and Pym had been peacefully sleeping. It had been easy to take that heavy ebony stick of his from near the window, so clearly visible in the moonlight, and strike before a single sound could escape her. Stealthily I had dragged her from the bed; Pym had continued sleeping.

And now? The chasm, of course! I seemed somehow to be highly elated with the gruesomeness of my mission, a mission totally foreign to my normal nature. Grimly I picked Betty Pym's limp body up in my arms, raised it over my head with unbelievable ease, then hurled it with all my strength into the eternal winds that rage and fume through that eight-hundred foot chasm. Immediately it vanished, lost to sight in the moonlight.

I threw myself down on my face and stared into the abyss. The wind stood my hair on end, whistled through my teeth. I was chilled to the bone. Still, I had accomplished my purpose, and that gave me a strange sense of complacency. Complacency for the implacable murder of a defenseless woman I hardly knew?

16

What sort of a dream was this? It was endowed with a vicious and transcending realism, far more vivid than any dream before; and yet I insisted to myself it was still a dream. That being so, I realized, from all the observations on dream psychology, that I ought to be awake. The realization of a dream being a dream immediately causes sleep to cease — but in this instance I went on dreaming!

Puzzled, I rose up at last and turned to look toward the silver streak of Coniston Water, my only link with the hotel. I moved forward, stumbled amid the countless stones. I was shivering and shaking both with cold and reaction, reeling and sprawling in ever-widening circles into the maw of a dank and inexplicable darkness . . .

I awoke suddenly, as though I had been forcibly thrown out of sleep into the waking world. The effects of that appalling nightmare were still upon me; relentless cold gripped my hands despite the warmth of the little bedroom. Shakily, I scrambled out of bed and connected the electric heater. By degrees, bathed in

17

the radius of its warmth, I began to feel more comfortable; the spasmodic twitching of my limbs ceased, the paralyzing sense of terror abated.

I sat there, wrapped in a blanket, my back against the foot of the bed, and gazed into the heart of the radiator's red-hot wires, trying to marshal some order out of the chaos in my mind. Once I got up and examined my shirt, trousers and shoes. A vast relief swept over me at discovering they were exactly where I had left them; the shoes were quite clean and bore no traces of the mud of the hillside. Satisfied, I crawled back into bed and slept again, without dreaming.

Awakening late in the morning, I dressed and shaved moodily, sneezed an absurd number of times, and finally made my way down to breakfast. Pym was already there, quietly eating bacon and eggs.

'You look tired, Moore,' he commented, surveying me. 'Didn't you sleep well?'

'I had a hell of a night,' I answered briefly. 'Must have been a cold coming on, I think. Awful dreams, too.'

'Awful dreams?' he repeated in vague surprise. 'How queer! Do you know, when I have a cold I don't dream at all. I seem to be drugged, in a sort of utter stupor. What did you dream about? Dreams interest me, you know.'

I looked at him steadily. 'I dreamt I stunned your wife with your heavy ebony walking stick, then murdered her by throwing her body from the top of Coniston Old Man into that chasm you pointed out last evening,'

'My dear fellow, you were in a bad way! A walk this morning will clear your head a bit, perhaps.'

'Incidentally,' I said, an odd feeling in my heart, 'where is your wife?'

'Oh, she went out for an early walk — she always does on holiday. Good Lord, Moore, you're not thinking that dream of yours was some sort of premonition? Or that it actually happened?'

'It — it was so vivid!' I muttered. 'Thank God I did only dream it!'

I began to eat, with this consolation in

my mind, but did not proceed very far. I was in no humour for food. I was about to rise when a hand suddenly fell upon my shoulder, and a voice, deep and strong, said:

'John Carlow Moore, I have a warrant for your arrest for the murder of Betty Pym . . .'

I twisted round, my heart thudding violently, and met the cold, grey eyes of a police inspector. Behind him in the doorway of the dining room stood two constables. Pym sat there opposite me, smiling strangely.

'Pym!' I gasped hoarsely. 'What does this mean?'

'It means, Moore,' he said grimly, 'that my wife's body was found in Dow Crag chasm, early this morning — by me! I went for a walk before dawn; I was unable to sleep and puzzled by her strange disappearance. I came upon her — horribly murdered. Naturally, I immediately notified the police; they were at work while you slept after your inhuman butchery. In my room were found an old tie of yours, a button from the shirt you wore, and your fingerprints on my ebony walking stick. It was a very simple matter to check them by the fingerprints on the bowl of your pipe up on the mantelpiece there. I persuaded the Inspector here that I could probably extract a confession from you, and I was more than successful, even though you did say it was a dream. A dream! My dear Moore!'

'But — but it was a dream!' I shouted huskily. 'Damn it, you told me yourself that your wife was out walking — '

'Only to lead you on. I soon guessed that you were the culprit; you told me yesterday that you hated my wife!'

I opened my mouth to speak, but the words refused to form. My mind became a tumbling chaos of confused thoughts. I was dimly aware of being hustled from that dining room and thrust, God knows how long after, into jail. Then, and only then, did my mind readjust itself. I secured the best defence I could and prayed for a satisfactory result. Poor fool that I was!

Only once did Pym visit me. He was smooth and collected as ever, his pale blue eyes shining brightly — but I knew him at last for the devil he really was. Yet I let him talk, and I listened.

'I felt that I should make it clear to you, my dear Moore, that I owe you no personal grudge. You have helped me wonderfully — proved the validity of the notion I told you about. My experiment, you see, was to discover if a man could commit murder without himself being anything but the mental agent behind it. It worked — admirably! My wife, you perhaps have realized, was prone to clandestine meetings with another man. I considered the problem very carefully from the moment I realized her unfaithfulness to me, and arrived at the conclusion that he was not nearly so much to blame as she. She was deceiving both him and me; therefore, she was better exterminated. Do I make myself clear?'

'You make yourself clear as a cold-blooded, incarnate devil!' I told him.

'Dear me; how very crude, Moore! However, I came to the Lake District to find a labourer or someone who would have done equally well as my tool; but it so happened I came upon you, so naturally I used you.'

'Go on!' I said, bitterly.

'I hypnotized you, Moore — completely. You remember the glitter of the tea-things when I told you that you would hate my wife? You remember the glare of the sun in your eyes when I told you that a body falling into Dow Crag chasm would be destroyed? You remember the heavy ebony stick I used to point out the landmarks? A complete sequence of events was hypnotically in your mind: hatred for my wife, the weapon for attack, and the place for the body . . .

'Last night you did everything I had commanded. I was not asleep when you stunned my wife. I followed you to the top of the mountain and back again, holding you under hypnotic control all the time. I saw what you did with my wife; I followed you back to the hotel. Needless to relate, I cleaned your shoes and rearranged your clothing to reassure your perhaps puzzled mind. It was I, too, who provided the clues in my room that led to your arrest, So very simple, you see!'

'You won't get away with it!' I vowed, thickly. 'I'll do all I can to bring you to book!'

'As you will,' he shrugged. 'So far as I am concerned, the world is rid of a very evil and designing woman. As for you, I am seeing to it that a good motive for your crime is supplied. You see, I am naming you as the other man. Maybe a little unfair of me, but very necessary . . . But my time is up, Mr. Moore. I will wish you good day, and — ' he gave a twisted smiled — 'good luck!'

Quietly he left the cell . . .

★   ★   ★

Need I dwell on the harrowing details of the events that ensued? I stood no earthly chance at the trial — Pym saw to that! All my efforts to prove the case one of hypnotic control failed completely. A matter-of-fact judge and jury were not impressed by my story of excursions into the mesmeric world; rather, they regarded it as a deliberate fabrication to shield my guilt. I only blackened my case by resorting to the truth . . .

As for Pym, he swore my soul away with a merciless implacability, aided by the extremely clever lawyer for the prosecution. I was found guilty and sentenced to death — a death whose details are mercifully hazy in my mind. But of the events following my death I have a very clear recollection . . .

I was buoyed up into the midst of a vast and embracing darkness, in which all concept of my other life and body vanished completely. I never saw any trace of my mortal body again. I was alone in a world of utter silence, yet filled with a thousand thoughts and conceptions that I could only assume were the mental radiations of the living people in the everyday world so utterly hidden from me. There was no real conviction of loneliness, just that all-pervading sensation of being the recipient of constant thoughts. Some were vague, some distinct, and at last I began to realize that these latter were connected with psychic and clairvoyant individuals. In this wise I encountered the mediumistic abilities of Henry Clifton, and through him I have succeeded in giving the story of my innocent part in what became known, so he advises me, as the 'Cumberland Horror.'

But there are last words to add to this narration. I am dead? No! My body is dead, but my mind lives on, and in such capacity I have exacted my revenge for the terrible thing that befell my earthly frame. Perhaps it was chance, or some instinctive mental gravitation, that caused me in my timeless wanderings to contact, finally, the mental vibrations of Enoch Pym himself. His thoughts, his every mental facet, were bared to my extra-mundane perceptions.

I gathered that he was in London, pursuing psychic and spiritualistic experiments, indulging in hypnotism, and generally turning hallowed and cherished concepts into a turmoil of diabolical villainy. He had found my vanquishing so simple that he was planning his hypnotic efforts on a larger scale, overpowering leaders of commerce and finance with his fascinating personality and ruthless mind. I perceived in him a mass-murderer, and therein also beheld my duty — and my own vengeance!

For interminable periods I held his mind in bondage, until the time came when I could strike. It came at one of his seances. I fought his hypnotic power with all the terrific energy of my free mind, until at last I felt opposition snap like the breaking of a bough in the wind and the emptiness of my eternal wanderings was devoid of all disturbing influences. The mentality of Pym had gone; and yet he could not be dead, surely, or I would have felt his presence in the after-life.

No, he was not dead. Clifton has told me that he became suddenly insane and babbles even now about a man named John Carlow Moore and a murdered woman on top of a mountain . . . Truly, then, I am avenged. I have gained a lasting and eternal peace, and am free to move endlessly in these swarming currents of mental vibration. Free — gloriously alone, and yet — unafraid!

2

Death at the Observatory

Jackson, janitor of the new Richmond Observatory, heard it first — a hoarse scream from down the passage leading to the main astronomical observatory. A scream, and then a babbling stream of words in which he recognized the voice of Dr. James Crayson, chief of the astronomical staff. Then, silence.

Jackson blinked, then dropped his mop with a wet thud on the linoleum and raced up the corridor at top speed, bursting in through the great green baize doors at the end.

An astounding sight met his eyes.

Dr. Crayson lay huddled on the floor, sprawled below the platform of the mighty new 400-inch reflector. Standing over him, a slender bright bar in his hand, was young Charles Bradmore, Crayson's assistant.

'Mr. Bradmore, sir, what's happened?'

As he gasped out the words Jackson slowly went forward, his eyes wide, fixed in horror on the motionless figure of the astronomer. With a sudden start he noticed the smear of blood from the doctor's dark head.

'You — you killed him!' he shrieked suddenly. 'Mr. Bradmore, you've gone and — '

'Oh, shut up!' Bradmore snapped. His young face was white, his fair hair dishevelled. 'Don't jump to such idiotic conclusions, man! Dr. Crayson fell from the platform, struck his head on this bar and it snapped off. He — ' He broke off. 'Where are you going?' he demanded, as Jackson swung around.

'Police!' the janitor howled, tearing out of the observatory. 'Police! Help! There's been a murder!'

His shouts brought other technicians from their night work in the great building. They crowded into the observatory, each adding his own opinion, each infuriating the haggard Bradmore all the more.

'You and Crayson never were on friendly terms, were you?' asked Dalroyd, the chief spectrographist in his cold, cynical voice. 'This looks pretty ugly for you, Bradmore.'

'Oh, shut up — all of you!' Bradmore blazed, his blue eyes flaming. 'I tell you he fell! He — '

'Nonetheless,' said Dalroyd steadily, 'this is a matter for the police.' And he strode through the assembly to the telephone.

The confused Bradmore hardly remembered what happened after that. He recollected the doctor saying that Crayson had died from a violent blow on the temple; he remembered, too, that he was asked a barrage of questions when the police arrived. Then, with relentless inevitability, the law took its course.

Bradmore, totally confused by the speed with which matters moved, had only a weak defence, and certainly no alibi. Circumstantial evidence piled up against him.

The observatory staff was bound to testify that it was well known Bradmore had little love for his superior, Crayson. Their work had always been done in a certain atmosphere of tension.

Bradmore knew full well that Crayson's job would have been his, except for influence in the background.

Wordy arguments between them had ensued many a time. And on this particular night . . .

The prosecuting counsel was certain of Bradmore's guilt. In a fit of anger Bradmore had smashed off the slender guide bar of the great telescope and dealt the astronomer a mortal, cowardly blow.

The only fingerprints on the bar were those of Bradmore. Crayson had not even touched it that evening. In vain Bradmore protested that Crayson had had no need to touch it; that he had picked it up when Crayson had smashed it off in his fall.

All too flimsy. The jury was only away twelve minutes and returned with the verdict of 'Guilty!'

The newspapers carried the story under the headline of 'Observatory Mystery'. But not a soul in the land, save one, believed that Bradmore was innocent. That one was his closest friend, Dick Warland.

Warland heard the whole case through, was even a witness to his friend's unimpeachable character. The jury's verdict was a terrific blow to him.

Then gradually out of the maze of his despair there came the slow beginnings of an idea. Was it possible that . . .

He reached for his coat and left his modest apartments in Golden Green at something closely approaching a run, on his way to see the one man who could help him — Scott Marlo, who had an enviable reputation for solving mysteries through scientific deductions.

Many in the scientific world said that Scott Marlo was crazy when he had forsaken an undoubtedly brilliant scientific career for the further pursuance of his hobby, criminology. Few credited his assertion that there was more scientific discovery in the unearthing of modern crime than there was in straight laboratory science.

The modern criminal, he averred, used scientific methods. He, Marlo, had set himself up against this vicious element, with remarkable success so far, even if Scotland Yard was at times prone to regard him as something of a dabbler.

His apartments over an Oxford Street store were large and well furnished, and carried a peculiar reek of chemicals. To the rear he had a complicated laboratory. Most of his time was spent in intricate analysis, using his masterful scientific mind for the extension of known theories into quite new channels, usually to the undoing of some criminal.

On the evening of Bradmore's conviction, Dick Warland was shown into the presence of this thirty-five-year-old scientist. The manservant left him alone in a quiet room in which the London traffic roar was muted, then Marlo appeared in a white smock.

Short, big-headed, square-jawed, with closely cropped black hair, he was unquestionably a man of action and swift decisions. As the scientist shook hands with him, Warland had a curious impression of rock-like strength and imperturbability, founded on definite knowledge.

Marlo's keen gray eyes were asking

questions all the time Warland stated his business.

'The Bradmore case?' Marlo repeated at last, after pondering a moment. 'Ah, yes. I have the facts tabulated. Very interesting, too. It was especially interesting to me as a scientific matter — astronomical, I mean . . . But why do you come to me?'

'Because I believe Bradmore is no more guilty than you or I — and I want you to use your knowledge in proving it.' Warland smiled a little apologetically. 'Unfortunately, I'm not a moneyed man. I can only pay modestly for your services. I've come to you because you are definitely the last hope. I believe something happened in that observatory of which nobody — not even Bradmore — had any knowledge. I believe that whatever it was accounted for Crayson's death.'

Marlo stroked his square chin with acid-stained fingers.

'Well, maybe,' he admitted finally. 'But that hardly justifies my butting in. I am not a professional criminologist — only an amateur.'

'But you're a scientist!' Warland cried

earnestly. 'This needs a man of science — not a detective. Nothing but a scientific cause could have killed Crayson. I'm convinced of it.'

'Ummm,' Marlo grunted, and pondered again. Then he started to walk round the room, thumping his fist in his palm. 'You know,' he said slowly, 'the more you recall the facts of the trial to my mind the more I begin to see your viewpoint. I thought at the time that there seemed to be certain weaknesses. A four-hundred-inch telescope, for instance, only newly installed — the greatest telescope ever made. Come to think of it, it might be worthwhile looking into the case if only to get a close look at that monster.'

'Whatever your reason,' urged Warland, 'I beg of you to look into it. But again, in all fairness, I must remind you that the money — '

'Money?' Marlo laughed shortly. 'What is it, anyway? Paper currency based on Element Seventy-nine — gold. I've no time for money. Got loads of it.' Again he hesitated, then his big dark head nodded slowly. 'Very well, I will look into it,' he promised quietly. 'But first of all there are one or two details I must arrange. My friend, Detective-Inspector Hartley, of Scotland Yard arranges official details for me, which allows me a permit as a free operator. In the meantime I shall study the situation.'

'And what must I do?' Warland demanded quickly.

'You? Nothing at all. Be at the Richmond Observatory, main entrance tomorrow night at eight. It will be dark then, and maybe that four-hundred-inch reflector will tell us something.'

Warland snatched his coat. 'Okay! Count on me! And thanks again and again. I'm going to get into touch with Bradmore and tell him all about it. Good night.'

Marlo didn't answer. He was already lost in thought, stabbing the air with his long index finger to emphasize certain points in his mind.

Scott Marlo kept his word. Warland, waiting on the observatory steps an hour before time, became aware of the scientist's stocky, powerful form striding through the misty darkness on the stroke of eight. He merely gave the briefest of nods, then strode purposefully into the main corridor, handed in his card, and moved on to the great, lighted observatory.

Warland found himself introduced to the bluff, plain-clothed figure of Inspector Hartley, and then to the technicians who had been summoned to attend.

'I don't know what I'd do without you, Hartley, to get things into shape,' Marlo commented, taking off his shaggy overcoat.

He rubbed and flexed his hands like a pianist about to play a concerto, then turned toward the mighty mass of the 400-inch reflector, stared thoughtfully on to the mirror screen immediately below it.

Most of it was covered with eiderdown. After a moment or two he mounted to the eight-feet-high platform from which Crayson had fallen, and sat down before the guiding eyepiece of the giant.

'Tell me,' he said, turning suddenly, 'what exactly was Dr. Crayson studying on the night he met his death? If any of you here know, please be absolutely exact.'

'I can tell you,' answered Dalroyd, coming forward. 'He was making an analysis of Sirius. There was some slight alteration in the star's magnitude and he was preparing to make a complete report. I know that because I was standing by ready to make spectroheliograph observations.'

'Sirius, eh?' Marlo's eyes narrowed. 'Sirius — the brightest star in the sky . . . How do you fix this telescope on any star? Eyepieces, or what?'

'Usually it is done by mathematical prearrangement, a science of angles. Only way to shift a giant like this. Then there is a preliminary survey through pilot telescopes for centring.'

'I see. Well, I'd be glad if you'd fix it on Sirius, now.'

Dalroyd nodded, motioned to two other technicians beside him, then they went to work together on the operation of massive controls and switchboards. The mammoth contrivance moved slowly in its great gimbals, was adjusted to a hair fineness of focus, and finally was trained on to the mirroid reflector from which the eiderdown was removed.

Marlo, Warland, and Hartley stood with the others, staring down into the mirror. Sirius was dazzlingly reproduced, the mistiness of the upper atmosphere creating but little disturbance. For a long time Marlo stood frowning and making notes.

'Well, nothing unusual there,' he muttered. 'Except for the star's savage brightness, which may have something to do with the matter.'

He debated again then, apparently struck by a sudden thought, climbed the trellis work of the reflector and examined it closely.

'And nothing there either,' he said, descending again. 'It had occurred to me that some device, actuated by light waves from Sirius on a selenium cell might have been attached to this reflector — some kind of apparatus designed to give Crayson a mortal blow, afterward to be cleared by the guilty party. But there's no sign of anything.'

'What did you expect — a sledge-hammer?' asked Dalroyd coldly.

Marlo ignored the sarcasm, stood musing.

'Don't you think you're all wrong this time, Marlo?' Hartley asked patiently. 'After all, all this is quite unorthodox, with the case closed. And besides, we — '

'If we find definite evidence to prove Bradmore's innocence it doesn't matter a lot if the case is closed or not,' Marlo retorted. 'Keep quiet a minute.'

Oblivious of everybody he started to walk round slowly, jabbing his finger in the air.

'Sirius, three weeks ago,' he muttered. 'Spin of the earth . . . distance covered — Hmmm . . . ' He stood staring in front of him, then suddenly he swung round and snatched his coat.

'That's all for now,' he said shortly. 'Thanks for your help. Good night!'

'Hey, wait a minute!' Warland cried, racing after him as he made for the door. 'What line are you working on? Can't you give me some idea?'

Marlo shrugged. 'Don't know myself

yet. Maybe hit or miss. Have to work it out in my laboratory.'

'Can't I come with you?'

'Nothing stopping you, is there? Come on.'

It was close on eleven by the time they got back to Oxford Street, and once within his rooms Marlo began to reveal something of the real dynamic energy in his makeup. Without even a suggestion of refreshment or idea of sleep he sat down at his desk, switched on the light directly over it and started to figure rapidly on a thick notepad.

Warland could only lounge in a chair and watch, totally in the dark as to what was going on. Here and there Marlo gave a few hints, but they were vague.

'On the night Crayson died there was something different about Sirius to what we saw tonight,' he said at last, after nearly two hours of note-making. 'I'm satisfied as to that. What I have to do is to work out the distance Earth has travelled since Crayson studied Sirius. According to my calculations the position now is that we would have to look at the star

Zaurac in order to look through the same portion of space that Crayson looked through. You understand?'

'Yes.' Warland nodded. 'But what does it prove?'

'I don't know — yet.'

Marlo debated a moment, then got to his feet and led the way into the adjoining laboratory. Pressing a button in the wall he sent a portion of the room sliding aside, manoeuvered a small but powerful telescope into position. He only stared into the eyepiece for a moment or two, then visibly winced. It was clearly a supreme effort to tear his gaze away.

Warland stared at him in astonishment. The scientist had dropped into a chair, his face drawn and white, his hands trembling.

'Heavens!' he whispered. 'Good Heavens!'

'But what — ' Warland began, then strode to the instrument and seized it.

To his surprise Marlo sprang up and whirled him back, thumbed the switch that sent the roof portion back into place.

'Don't look!' he breathed, fighting for

calm. 'Don't look!' He took a deep breath, then said slowly, 'You can take it from me, Warland, that the innocence of Bradmore can be definitely established. Now I know what killed Crayson!'

'What?' Warland demanded.

'You'll know the instant I have gathered together officials from the right quarter. You be at Richmond Observatory again, two nights from now, and then — ' Marlo stopped, held out his hand. 'Good night, Warland. See you Thursday at eight o'clock.'

Warland took the dismissal quietly, went out into the quiet street, his hopes buoyed, though he did wonder what Marlo had seen . . .

★   ★   ★

It was clear that in the two-day interval Marlo had pulled several influential strings, for when Warland arrived in the observatory he found not only the scientist himself and Inspector Hartley, but — among other experts — Judge Milbank, who had sat in the Bradmore case.

After introductions, Marlo moved to the platform of the giant telescope, stood surveying his audience and gripped the handrail in front of him.

'Gentlemen, I intend to put before you tonight certain facts, together with a demonstration, to prove indubitably that Charles Bradmore did not kill Dr. James Crayson. Let us begin at the beginning.

'In the first place, Bradmore was found with a metal bar in his hand. Evidence at the trial showed it had his fingerprints upon it. Evidence also proved that the bar was one of the many small guider rods of this gigantic reflector which could be easily smashed off by a heavy blow. Crayson's fingerprints were not on it because on the night in question he had had no reason to handle it.

'Bradmore, as assistant astronomer, set the telescope to the desired spot by instruments. That desired spot was the star Sirius. Also, Bradmore handled the bar afterward. That accounts for his fingerprints. In the interval the telescope moved by its own machinery, of course, to keep pace with the Earth's movement through space and regular rotation upon its axis.

'I submit, gentlemen, that Bradmore's statement was true in every detail. Dr. Crayson did fall from this platform, and in so doing struck his head on the bar. The bar snapped off. Bradmore picked it up; quite a natural thing to do in the circumstances — and was thus found by the janitor. Bradmore's personal dislike of Crayson, other facts of his private life, finally led to a conviction.'

The audience remained silent. Some of them were looking doubtful.

'Crayson died because of what he saw through this telescope,' Marlo resumed in a steady voice. 'Let me show you, gentlemen — and I warn you to keep control over yourselves.'

He glanced at his notes then turned to Dalroyd. 'Fix this telescope on the star Mira,' he ordered quietly. 'And do it without any direct observations. I have my reasons.'

Dalroyd and his two assistants nodded and set to work. It took them seven minutes to fix the position by the precision instruments. Marlo finally nodded, gave a signal, and the lights were lowered.

The group sat motionless, watching the mammoth reflector. Marlo fingered the main switches carefully and the mirror came slowly into life.

But it was not the pulsing, variable light of Mira upon which the men gazed. Instead they found themselves held rigidly transfixed by a blaze of hideous, interwoven colours — blinding radiances of all hues.

The colours themselves were awful enough, but the effect they produced was even worse. They exerted a fascinating mesmerism, forced the mind from its ordinary channels into one of frozen panic, then into a growing sense of unbelievable terror.

The effect heightened. An unbearable tension began to gather. 'Stop it!' screamed Dalroyd suddenly. 'Stop! In Heaven's name, stop!'

With an effort, Marlo switched off. The lights came up. It was several minutes before any of the party recovered, and even then they were white-faced and shaken.

'Gentlemen,' Marlo breathed at last,

'you saw that vision over the wide area of the mirror. For that reason its effect was not nearly so potent as on the night Crayson saw it through an eyepiece. He got the concentrated force of it, and the star he was looking at was the strongest star in the whole sky — Sirius. Infinitely brighter than the one we viewed tonight, or the one I viewed myself.'

'But what does it mean?' demanded Dalroyd, mopping his brow. 'What's wrong with the star? Or is it the reflector itself?'

'Neither. The trouble is in space.' Marlo hesitated, as though marshalling his facts, then proceeded: 'Space, so far as we can ascertain, is the carrier of electrons, which in themselves carry radiations of varied types. The word 'medium' is here appropriate. Now, as a small example. When electrons change position in, say, the Sun, they give forth energy in the course of their displacement.

'That energy travels through space, displaces electrons in our eyes and gives rise to the sensation of sight. We say: 'I see the Sun's light.' Naturally, this electronic change is responsible for everything we see. Normally, there is nothing in space to prevent electronic change producing its customary effect of light. But a spatial *warp*, the slightest bending of these light waves from the normal wave length which produces white light can instead split it up into prismatic colours by alterations of wave length. It can do more.

'A human eye, tuned to accept certain colours and wave lengths, is utterly at variance when suddenly faced with a series of vibrations it has never known. What happens? The brain revolts against these new sensations in its effort to master them, even as the body itself revolts, and dies, in the effort to assimilate poison instead of normal food. What happened then, was this: Out in space there is a warp, a slight bending or pucker in the fabric of space which, in one quarter of space, has changed visible light into a combination of colours destructive to the brain if received in full force.

'How that warp came about we cannot know. It may be the outcome of interwoven vibratory forces of which we know less than nothing — but we do know that the unfortunate Crayson viewed Sirius when that space warp was right between him and the star.

'With such a telescope as this he got the full blast of unfamiliar wave lengths. He went instantly insane. He fell, screaming, smashed his head against the telescope bar and . . . well, that was what killed Crayson.

'And my own conclusions? The details showed me that only a space warp could be possible. Astronomy is one of my many lines of thought and, as I worked, I remembered that somewhere I had read a treatise on space warps and their manifestations, together with the suggestion that the extraordinary variability of some of the fixed stars might be accounted for by such warps.

'The basis of a warp could clearly, magnified by a reflector like this, cause instant death. I began to see what had happened. But how to prove it? Presumably the warp was stationary, forming in one spot and dissolving in that spot as fresh radiations took its place. I learned what star Crayson had studied on the night of his death. From that I had to work out, by mathematics, the speed of the Earth's journey through space and the relative change in positions compared to the cosmos, and so finally arrived at the approximate point in the sky where the space warp ought still to be on view.

'I found it. I studied Zaurac, a comparatively weak star, through a likewise weak telescope, but even at that I experienced considerable mental turmoil. Young Warland here will verify that. The rest was more mathematics — the sorting out of where the warp would be tonight; namely, in front of Mira. You saw what happened. Also in the meantime I advised other astronomers, through the courtesy of the Astronomer Royal, to refrain from viewing the heavens in specialized points until we had had a consultation.

'Any of them might have met the same fate as Crayson, but Providence stayed their hand in looking through that warped space. In time, the warp will dissolve. Until then, precautions will be taken. In space, then, gentlemen, is the real culprit, entirely beyond our jurisdiction. As for me, I will stand witness at a reopening of the trial, and I have the support of the Astronomer Royal, and you gentlemen here tonight.'

A silence fell on the group as Marlo stopped talking. Then at length he walked down from the platform and Judge Milbank rose to his feet.

'There's not the slightest doubt, Marlo, that you have accomplished a scientific deduction of phenomenal brilliance,' he said quietly. 'What's more, you proved it. I have little doubt as to the outcome.'

He nodded gravely to the others and walked out. Warland swung around and gripped Marlo's hand eagerly.

'I can't begin to thank you!' he choked. 'If you'll let me have your bill — '

'Bill?' Marlo frowned. 'Oh, that! Be hanged to it. No use for money. Got too much of it.' He stood regarding Warland thoughtfully. 'Just the same,' he added slowly, 'I could do with somebody like you to help me now and again. My activities may extend after the publicity from this case. What about it?'

'You mean it?' Warland cried in joyful amazement.

But Marlo was already at the door getting into his coat.

'Course I mean it!' he snapped. 'What are we waiting for? Come on, man!'

3

Judgment Bell

I had noticed the storm gathering for some time. During the afternoon while Enid Cleggy and I had picnicked amidst a carpet of green grass and buttercups, the heat had taken on a certain sullen, crushing load. It had become an effort to even move, so we had lain on our backs and gazed at the drowsy June sky, watching the slow but imperceptible gathering of deep smoky-blue clouds on the southern horizon.

Towards late afternoon quiet had fallen over the rolling landscape of this southern English countryside. Far away, cows stood with their backs to the hedges. This in itself was significant.

'Enid, we'd better be moving,' I said at last, anxiously. 'We have not the car, remember, and if we want to finish the day out in dry clothes we had better get moving for the 'bus. And that's three miles! Come on.'

Enid nodded and helped me to pack up the picnic tackle into the wicker basket, then carrying it between us we hurried across the grass on the return journey to the 'bus stop.

Altogether though, despite this abrupt finish, it had been a grand day, one of the very few I was able to permit myself from a busy life in the city. Enid, too, had arranged it so that she could accompany me, for as the head saleswoman of a London dress salon she had little time to spare.

She was a practical sort of girl, good-looking in a sharp kind of way, with blonde hair and keen grey eyes. Never in so many actual words had we admitted to each other that we were in love. It was accepted for granted, as so often happens between busy people — but I was resolved it should not be long before I asked her to become my wife.

'It's raining!' she exclaimed suddenly, holding out her palm.

It was — big drops. The storm clouds

had gathered now from blue to violet. Far away in the distance was a crumbling, rolling thud that marked the storm's overture: and now came a strange thing. During all this summer day I had been blissfully happy, yet with the first growl of distant thunder something happened to me.

An indescribable sensation of dread seized upon me, a sense of withering foreboding. I just could not understand it. After all, I had never been afraid of thunderstorms — not afraid of anything, indeed. Yet —

'What's the matter, Bob?' Enid asked the question in surprise.

I gave a start, forced a smile. 'Eh? Oh — nothing. Just felt a bit strange, as though — Skip it,' I growled. 'Probably the electric tension before the storm breaks.'

'Or those sardines,' she reflected. 'I had my doubts about them at the time — Say, we must hurry,' she added in anxiety. 'The rain's increasing and we're only wearing thin things.'

We broke into a run as the rain came

down harder. Soon it was hissing all round us, bubbling in the dry, sun-scorched grass, sending a miasma of steam floating up from the valley atop which rolled this undulating country. The further we went the more apparent it became to me that we could never reach the 'bus stop, much less home, without being drenched to the skin. Yet if we sheltered under one or other of the dotted trees we would be just asking for it.

I slid to a standstill in the muddy grass, rain beating on my bare head. Enid stopped too, her flimsy frock plastered to her slender form, and her hair a dripping mop.

'What about Kelby Abbey?' I suggested. 'It's only half a mile away in the dip there. It's always open. We could shelter.'

She hesitated; and I knew why. There is a legend about Kelby Abbey — but after all there are legends about all abbeys, more or less, especially one like Kelby, over five hundred years old.

'It'd be a sanctuary,' I went on earnestly. 'This looks like being the devil of a storm. We might be struck dead out here.'

'All right,' she agreed, but reluctantly. 'Frankly, I've never felt too happy about churches since my uncle dropped dead in one twelve years ago.'

It was no time to argue about this, so off we went as hard as we could go through slush and wet grass. As we went the first fiendish crack of thunder broke right over our heads simultaneously with the lightning. It was a terrific flash, drenching the storm-ridden land in bright blue.

Again with it came that sensation of unsupportable horror. It was a most terrible feeling, as though my soul had been momentarily plunged into a nethermost Pit of the Damned. I said nothing to Enid about it: she was alarmed enough already with the fury of the storm.

We ran like champion track sprinters along that last half mile, the picnic basket between us. The wind had risen by now and was bending and lashing the elms in a fury of gloom that had deepened into a near-twilight. Twice as we finished the course the lightning whip-lashed across the ebon sky and the thunder set the ground quaking; then through the haze of rain loomed the ponderous semi-ruined bulk of Kelby Abbey, with its ever-open door.

We floundered up the steps and into the quiet, sombre interior. Peace dropped upon us immediately like a mantle. We paused a while, put the basket down, glanced back at the rain hissing down on the worn steps. We thanked God on that moment for Kelby Abbey with its doors ever open to the devout who might seek its hallowed precincts for a brief relief from the life material.

Enid gave a rather relieved smile.

'Well, we are out of that, anyway . . . Might be as good a chance as any to look at this place. I've seen it from the outside many a time, only I'm afraid I have not been interested enough — or religious enough — to look inside. Let's see, this is the modern part isn't it? This porch-way? And the rest is restored ancient abbey, with the real ruins at the far back. Hmm, might as well start reforming. Coming?'

For some reason her words sounded cold and worldly in this mighty place. This was one thing I could never quite fathom about Enid. Somewhere deep in her character there ran a streak of cold, frigid cynicism. It leapt to the surface every time she was confronted with something hallowed. Yet, knowing she had had to make her own way in the world, knowing she had all the sophistication a great modern city could instill into her, I had always ignored this brazen facet in her character. After all, I am no saint myself . . .

Turning, we gazed into the church itself down the nave. At the moment it was plunged into the twilight of the storm, but suddenly lightning came again and gave us a blue-lit impression of enormous stained glass windows, mighty stone pillars, carven saints, empty pews, and at the far end the choir-tiers and altar.

Enid gave a sudden little shiver. 'Cold,' she muttered. 'All churches are cold, especially ancient ones like this. Besides, I'm wet . . . '

She wrung out the hems of her sleeves and skirt impatiently, shivered again as draught came hurtling through the open door. Finally, driven by curiosity, she went wandering along the nave into the dead emptiness of the church. I went after her, followed her past the mighty altar, through a passage and so into the cloisters. Here, though, one side open to the storm, we beat a hasty retreat. But not into the church. We opened an oak door and passed quickly into what we took to be a kind of ante-chamber.

It was some kind of crypt, however, or else a storehouse, since a crypt is usually below ground. Certainly it was old, thick walled, and dusty. Lightning played violently on the solitary mullioned window, lighting up a bare deal table, a hardwood chair, and shelf upon shelf packed with musty files and books.

'Looks like some kind of monk's reading room,' I decided at length; then wandering forward I looked at the books on the shelves. With the lightning's help I made out some of the titles and found they were Latin. For the rest there seemed to be only Abbey files, no doubt packed with historical gems.

'Just what *is* the legend about this Abbey?' Enid asked at length, coming to my side and hugging herself to keep warm. 'Isn't it something about a bell? I've heard of it but I don't just seem to recall . . . Probably gossip anyway!'

'The legend,' I said, 'is that a giant bell rings out just before a death is to take place in this church. Always the death occurs in this Abbey. Last time it rang out was about twelve years ago, I think.'

Enid frowned. 'But surely they ring the bells on Sundays?'

'The ordinary ones, yes; but this other bell of the legend is a solitary one in a belfry all by itself. Erected for some special reason, when this place was first built, there were originally four bells in this special belfry; then three were taken away and one was left. It was called, and still is, the Judgment Bell.'

'Hmm, you sound like a guide,' Enid chided. 'Anyway, it sounds like a lot of bosh.'

She turned, disdainful, ran her eyes

over the files. It was as she looked at them and the lightning flashed again with savage brightness that the vast sense of evil domination swept me again. It was as though a nameless *Presence* — and that *Presence* unthinkably foul and Godless — were trying to overwhelm and crush me. Here, in the hallowed backwaters of the Abbey where even the thunder was muted by densely thick walls, the effect was infinitely greater than it had been outside.

An irresistible impulse led me to catch Enid's arm as she reached out towards the shelf. My grip was so tight she turned with a little cry.

'Bob — you're hurting me — !' Her voice was both pained and amazed.

I could feel that my face was a strained mask. With an effort I released her.

'Sorry,' I muttered, as the sensation flowed away from me again. 'Can't imagine what came over me — Sort of creepy feeling. Maybe it is this church, and the storm.'

'The church more like it,' she answered laconically. 'Enough to give anybody the blues. For some reason these places never make me feel holy; only irritated and resentful. Wonder why things that are sacrosanct have to be depressing and shadowy?'

She meditated briefly on this, then returning to the shelf she took down a file. It was as though she did it with a hand other than her own. It was an unerring movement, so unerring indeed she even seemed surprised herself, for she stood looking in the dim light at the incredibly ancient dust-ridden thing in her hands.

'Now what on earth do I want this for?' she demanded. 'I was *going* to look at those books on the lower shelf to pass the time away and instead I — ' She shrugged. 'We'll have a look anyway.'

She flung the file on the bare wood table and dust flew in a cloud. At the same second a truly soul-racking crash of thunder broke over the Abbey, smashing its way along with the lightning that swamped us for a moment in blue fire. My head swam with the intensity of it. The hair on my scalp bristled for a second or two.

'Apparently coming right overhead,' I muttered. 'And so far as I know this Abbey is the only landmark for miles. A perfect target. Maybe we'd better get out?'

Enid glanced at the window down which the rain was swilling in cascades.

'Not for me. I feel as though I might get pneumonia even as it is. I'm taking no more chances.'

She turned back to the file and opened it. Dusty parchment pages flickered under her slender fingers. The ink, though faded, was still legible, most of it in old English writing style. I gazed over her shoulder, mastering an unformed desire to snatch the file from her and hurl it out into the storm. A silly idea, you say? Perhaps so, looked at impartially, but you can have no idea of the crushing forces at work upon me — and for all I knew then upon Enid too — in that stormbound church.

Why, for instance, had she decided to open that file at the exact page headed —

YE LEGENDE OF KELBYE ABBEY

'Well, how's that for luck?' she asked cynically. 'We were wondering about that old wives' tale — and here it is as large as life. But Lord, what impossible writing — ' She started to quote aloud, slowly . . . ' — *and so ye tale doth run that ye saintly monk Dranwold wert slain by the assassin's hand, who didst creep* — '

Enid broke off and sighed, 'Whew! Whoever wrote this sure wouldn't sell much to a modern magazine.'

'For Heaven's sake, Enid, stop your damned blasphemous chatter!' I exploded. 'Stop it, I say!'

She stared blankly at me. Those words had hurled themselves out of me; and the odd thing was that as I said them that sense of gnawing horror noticeably receded as though the sharp words had cowed it — whatever *it* was.

'Just who,' Enid asked bitterly, 'do you think you're talking to?'

'You, of course! What right have you to make fun of the hallowed files of this place? Don't you realize what that file is? It records the death of a monk — a holy, saintly man — who was murdered by an assassin! *That* isn't a subject for levity.'

I saw her lips quiver as she formed a

cutting reply; then she relaxed and gave a little shrug.

'The storm's getting into you, Bob. Never the less, all blasphemy aside, this stuff is queer to our modern sense. It looks as — '

She stopped, her eyes frozen to that ancient page. I don't think I ever saw such a look on a human face. It was horror beyond describing. Even another terrific flash of lightning failed to make her blink, so entranced was she.

'Enid, Enid, whatever is it?' I cried, clutching her. 'In God's name, why do you stare like that?'

Her hand rose slowly to her mouth in horror. Then with a vast effort she seemed to get a grip on herself again. She pointed to the page, traced a single line at the bottom of the Legend:-

... *and so shall ye Judgment Bell ring for each descendant of this assassin of Dranwold. This assassin whose name is Cleggye* ...

'Cleggy!' I gulped. 'Spelt in the old English style. But — but that's your surname, Enid.'

66

'Yes,' she whispered. 'Yes, it is.'

She looked at me with blank grey eyes for a moment. Her face had dewed with emotion in those few paralyzing moments. Now, with a hand that visibly trembled, she shut the file, fell quivering against the table.

'I don't understand it,' she panted, her breast rising and falling stormily. 'I don't understand — I feel lost in here, Oppressed! *Do you realize what this file says?*' she screamed.

'I realize that by a coincidence in names the assassin of monk Dranwold had the same surname as you.' I said. 'But after all, Enid, that might easily happen. Cleggy is a common name.'

'No, it isn't!' she countered flatly. 'Clegg, yes — and Clegger too — are good old fashioned English root names. Not Cleggy. That's definitely unusual . . . It means,' she finished, fighting to control herself, 'that assassin Cleggye was probably an ancestor of mine.'

'It's ridiculous — ' I started to say; then I stopped. *Was* it so ridiculous, after all? I recalled my own strange emotions, that sense of abysmal fear that had kept assailing me. Above all, I remembered how she had reached for that file almost automatically and had opened it at the desired place immediately . . .

We stared at each other as the lightning blazed again.

'Suppose,' Enid said slowly, at length, 'this is true? That this murderer *is* an ancestor of mine? What does it make me?'

'Only what you are,' I said, almost roughly. 'A modern girl in a modern world. It isn't possible that something that happened centuries ago could affect you now . . . '

She hesitated, then turned back to the file again. She read slowly, nervously, transcribing into modern English as she went —

' . . . 'Monk Dranwold was at prayer before the altar. Assassin Cleggye stole in from the region of the transept and stabbed him in the back . . . And his death shall be eternally avenged: such was the dying curse of Dranwold . . . ' *And his death shall be eternally avenged,*' Enid repeated slowly.

'All my ancestors and relations, as far back as I can remember, have died mysteriously . . . Bob!' Her voice was sharp with sudden hysteria. 'Bob, we're going to get out of here, and quickly. It was no mere chance that brought us here, I'm convinced — '

I was commencing to think the same thing. Was it possible, I wondered, that force of events — a force totally beyond our comprehension — had led us out on the picnic, had trapped us in the storm, and thence directed us — at any rate Enid — to this Abbey? Was it possible that there was a spirit of vast evil abroad in this storm, striving to reach the girl, a descendant of a Godless assassin? Was that sense of insupportable evil I had sensed somehow produced through *her*, the modem equivalent of Cleggye? I gave a little shudder.

'Yes, we'll go,' I said abruptly. 'Things are happening in this place which are beyond our ken. Come on!'

We hurried back through the rain-drenched cloisters into the ghostly recesses of the church, went along past the silent pews to the porch-way where our picnic basket still lay. Here, outside the main door, we paused.

The storm seemed to have centred with a demoniac fury directly over this ancient pile. Rain was pouring in through the open door in hissing sheets; lightning flashed and crackled in the deluge; the tear and rip of the thunderbolts shook the Abbey to its very foundations.

'We dare not go out in this,' I whispered. 'We just dare not. We'd be struck dead before we'd gone a dozen yards.'

'I don't understand this storm,' Enid whispered. 'It's as though the very elements have gone mad over this spot. It doesn't seem to move on as all storms should — Bob, I'm frightened.' She caught my arm tightly, and I felt her hand trembling.

'Take it easy,' I said, though I was not feeling any too heroic myself. 'It's just a violent summer storm, that's all — Pass off in a while. Then we'll get moving again. Still be plenty of time,' I added, glancing at my watch. 'It's only six o'clock as yet.'

'Six o'clock,' she echoed hollowly; 'and as dark as midnight.'

She wandered back again into the church fretfully, stared down the nave. Then as the lightning blazed across it she gave a terrific scream, so intense and horror-stricken I twirled with a thumping heart.

'What on earth — ?' I demanded, catching up with her.

'I — I saw him!' she chattered. 'I saw him — there before the altar. Oh, my God — I *saw him*!'

'Saw who?' I demanded, staring down the lightning-illuminated expanse and beholding nothing unusual.

'Dranwold! The monk. Kneeling at the altar — '

She was so prostrated with fright she could hardly stand up. I caught hold of her, held her tightly to me. She kept her eyes from looking into the church. I continued to hold her, her face pressed against my shoulder. Yet as I looked down the nave and each flash of chain-lightning filled the place I could see nothing unusual, certainly nothing to suggest a kneeling figure.

'There's nothing there,' I said gently; 'nothing at all. It was your imagination — shadows cast by the lightning, I expect. Your nerves are all shot to pieces by the storm and the legend, that's all . . . '

Slowly she forced herself to look again, then just as quickly jerked her head away.

'He *is* there — kneeling,' she insisted. 'In hood and cassock! Don't ask me to look again. I dare not — '

This time I did not deny her assertion. There was something very real, very terrible, which she could see and yet I could not. Involuntarily my mind went back to the filed legend. Hereditary influence? The assassin Cleggye operating through her?

Then there came back that sinking sense of overwhelming evil, so much so that I shrank from before it. It was as much as I could do to keep a grip on Enid. I wanted to hurl her away from me in loathing as though *she* were the cause of my sensations.

'It's gone now,' she said presently, straightening up. 'Yes — it's gone.' She stared wide-eyed down the nave at the distant lightning-bright altar. 'Perhaps . . . perhaps it *was* only a shadow.'

The way she said it convinced me she did not believe it. She knew she had seen something, and it left her badly shaken.

'Perhaps we'd better get back to our crypt,' I said.

She nodded assent so we stole back through the flashing, rumbling gloom, across the stretch of rain-lashed cloister, and so back into our sanctuary. Now we beheld the most incredible thing.

The file, which had been left open on the table at the legend, had gone. Automatically our eyes switched to the shelf. *It was back in place among the other files*.

'The figure I saw — the monk — he must have done it,' Enid said hoarsely. 'Only *he* could have done it.'

'Good Heavens, Enid, do you realize what you are saying?' I cried. 'You are suggesting a supernatural power returned the file to the shelf.'

'Yes — I am!' she declared fiercely. 'Oh, I know that ghosts are absurd; that phantoms can't happen — That's all right in the city; but here there is something different, a vast and malignant power abroad in this very storm. Trying to reach me. I know it is. Bob, I *know* it is. You've got to help me.'

'But what against?' I shouted. 'How can any man attempt to fight the impalpable?'

'You must help me to be strong,' she implored desperately; and it was horrible for me to see how completely all the worldly sophistication had been torn away from her.

'This storm is not a natural one: I can sense that now. In it is the age-long struggle between good and evil forces, the battle of spirits long dead to mortal eyes, still centred over this Abbey. The battle of Dranwold the monk with my remote ancestor Cleggye. I *know* that is the truth. Don't ask me *how* I know — Perhaps it is instinct, hereditary knowledge stirred by occult forces . . . But it is *there*.'

Slowly, in the light of her statement, I began to understand my own emotions. If indeed long-dead enmity was being fought out in the furious clash of the storm, it was equally possible — as I had already vaguely realized — that the spirit of Cleggye was alive again through Enid. And his evil power was doing everything possible to protect his own, to protect *her*. Therefore this force had tried to overwhelm me: it had prompted me to restrain her from reading that file so the truth about Cleggye would never be known. That was it. An unholy reincarnation in which the very elements themselves had a part.

'It is the eternal cry of vengeance,' Enid said in a hollow voice. 'Echoing down the centuries. And I am the pawn . . . '

She relaxed then against the hard table, somewhat calmer now she had solved the psychic implications of her plight. We stood in silence for a long time, our faces patterned by the unceasing rage of lightning as we gazed at each other.

'Perhaps,' I said, making an effort, 'if we ran out and took a chance we might get away from this storm? It only seems to be concentrated around here — '

'We cannot get away,' she replied, shaking her head dully. 'Surely you have realized it by now? Psychic compulsion, nothing more or less, brought us here. The same compulsion caused us to picnic near the Abbey — the same evil forces brought about a storm: we came here. And now . . . '

I forced myself out of this quagmire of inexplicable things. I took hold of Enid and shook her violently.

'Enid, do you realize what you are saying?' I shouted, over the roaring of the thunder. 'Do you realize to what ridiculous dimensions we have allowed our imaginations to wander? To a summer storm we have applied occult explanations: to a shadow we find — you find anyway — a monk who has been dead for centuries . . .

'We're a modern man and a modern woman, sheltering in an Abbey. The mere coincidence of a name cannot — *shall* not! — bring about the total defeat of our sanity. It's — it's just an attack of nerves.'

'No, Bob.' Her face was ashy grey. 'No; it is truth. There is too much in it for it to be just coincidence — '

Suddenly she stopped, the words

stricken from her lips. For the briefest moment the roaring of the thunder had died and there was a sepulchral, crushing calm. It flayed our tautened nerves like a whip — Then out of this vast unnatural hush came a sound — the deep, solemn clanging of a bell from somewhere over our heads. It tolled once — twice — three times, filling the very echoes with its quivering pure-cast strokes.

'Judgment Bell,' I hardly realized I said the words.

'No! *No! No!*' Enid screamed. 'I can't stand it, I can't — '

She flung herself to the crypt doorway as yet another stroke clanged through the gloomy silences. Then thunder rolled again; but the bell kept on chiming, relentlessly, implacably, though, so far as we knew, there was no human hand to toll it.

'Enid!' I shouted huskily: then I darted after her fleeing figure. She seemed to have gone demented with fright. Once she had gotten into the church again she went blundering along up the aisle between the pews, obviously making for the porch and outer door.

'*Enid!*' I yelled again, but she took no notice of me.

Then I drew up short as she suddenly halted midway up the church and threw up her hands as though to shut out some monstrous obscene vision. She wheeled, clearly visible to me in the lightning; she came racing back towards the altar as though Lucifer himself were behind her.

'Monk Dranwold!' she shrieked. 'Behind me. Seizing me — No! No!'

The echoes were brimming with her shouts and cries — the cries of the damned indeed. I was paralyzed with horror at the dreadful enactment going on, this pursuit of a helpless girl by something I could not even see.

Stumbling, gasping, I saw her at last on her knees before the altar.

'Mercy!' she gasped helplessly. 'In God's name — mercy — '

Abruptly, I found myself and jumped forward, determined to seize her by force and get her out of this damnable hole; but at that very moment there came a flash of lightning such as I had never known.

A blinding purple fork stabbed clean through the mighty stained window at one side of the altar, splintering it instantly. For the briefest moment I saw Enid crouched in frozen terror on the very spot where centuries before Dranwold had been slain at prayer — Then that terrible sizzling bolt struck clean upon Enid.

The awful shock to my nerves sent me reeling helplessly, my ears stunned by the most unholy din. Thunder, the clamour of the Judgment Bell, the noise of splitting stone and Enid's dying shriek were all woven together.

Sickened, half-blinded by the flash, I went reeling forward, caught her body up in my arms. It was a terrible sight upon which I gazed. One half of her body was charred to the bone!

'Enid!' I screamed. 'Enid — '

The absurdity of shouting to this poor, dead, blackened corpse blasted in upon me. I lowered her again gently, sprang up with my fists clenched. What inhuman devilry was going on in here?

'Fiend!' I shrieked. 'Fiend! Wherever

you are come out and face me. Come *out*, I say — '

Silence — utter silence. The clanging of the giant bell had ceased now: even the thunder seemed to have died away miraculously. The blinding flashes of lightning were beginning to lose their power; through the smashed window I saw a clearing streak in the violet of the storm clouds.

'Trickery.' I spat the word out. 'Filthy trickery. Some escaped lunatic is in this place; he slew Enid — '

I think, from the things I said, that I was half crazy with fear and grief. I remember I went tearing around looking for a way to the belfry, and at last I found it — ancient stone steps. I hurtled up them three at a time, swung open the unbolted door and stepped inside. It was empty, ropes swinging in the fresh wind blowing through open windows.

What was I thinking, of, anyway? The Judgment Bell had a separate belfry. Of course! I wheeled and went to the only other door at this high point of the Abbey. It was locked. I slammed on it with bruised and bleeding fists.

'Devil of devils, come out!' I thundered. 'Come out! You shall not escape me — !'

I thumped and kicked and yelled until my heart felt as though it would burst from exertion and hysteria. Gulping, I fell back against the wall, my head whirling. Then I stiffened as I caught the sound of footsteps on the stone staircase. I waited, my fingers outspread like claws . . .

The footsteps came nearer — slow and deliberate. They stopped suddenly — Yet it was no other-world visitor upon which I gazed, no demoniac being or a monk in hood and shroud, but a man in soft hat and dripping mackintosh. He came towards me slowly, and I saw he had a very pale, drawn face.

'My dear man, whatever are you doing here?' he asked in wonder. Then his face saddened a little. 'But I think I can guess. That poor girl below, by the altar — She was struck by lightning?'

'Either that or there's some brutally clever trickery going on in this place,' I grated back. 'Who the devil are you, anyway?'

'I am David Bolton, Vicar of this Abbey,' he answered quietly. 'I heard the clanging of the Judgment Bell. But then' — he gave a little shrug — 'I expected it when I saw the storm had come again.'

'Again?' I echoed, startled. 'It has been — before?'

'Yes; twelve years ago.' His voice was very quiet, 'That time a man died in very similar circumstances to that girl below. The Abbey was struck by lightning while he and a party of friends were sheltering. He was the victim of electric shock. His name . . . was Roland Cleggy.'

I stared at the Vicar with gaping mouth. I was remembering that Enid had said her Uncle had dropped dead in a church twelve years before. At that time she would have been too young to knew the full circumstances and — .

'This girl,' the Vicar said. 'She too was named Cleggy?'

I nodded stupidly.

'So,' he muttered, 'it will always be, until every descendant of the accursed Cleggye is destroyed. Five have died in this very Abbey, through the centuries.

Others will die here, too — forced here by occult power — unless that girl was the last of the line. We cannot deal with things like this, my friend — they are the powers of Darkness. The Monk Dranwold, as he died, placed an everlasting curse of retribution upon his assassin and successors. Always the curse has stricken down. There is always the Storm — a terrible Storm — in which the soul of Cleggy and the curse of Dranwold are still at grips; but always a Cleggy is vanquished . . . '

He laid a gentle hand on my arm.

'From records of past deaths I can imagine just what must have happened. You were directed by unseen powers to the crypt wherein lie the Abbey files. There the girl saw the Legend. Later, perhaps, she would imagine she saw the ghost of Dranwold himself praying at the altar. When at last she was stricken down where Dranwold himself died the powers of darkness abated; the Storm began to recede. The Judgment Bell ceased its tolling . . . '

'It isn't true, any of it!' I cried suddenly.

'It *is* true,' he stated quietly. 'Implacably true, but in a setting you or I can never understand this side of Eternity.'

'Human agency rang that damned Judgment Bell,' I shouted. 'It was not one of the ordinary bells: it had a different sound — I say Enid Cleggy was murdered, that perhaps the lightning was — was a flash of magnesium or something. I demand to see inside this Judgment Bell belfry. It's the last hiding place and the door is locked!'

He smiled gravely. 'The power that put the file back on its shelf also rang this bell,' he said.

'How did you know about the file?' I flashed at him.

'I know because it has always happened the same way. However, you shall have your wish granted. Just a moment.'

He went downstairs and obtained a massive key, came back and, twisted it in the door lock. The door swung open. But this — the last and only hiding place — was empty.

'To the world,' said the Vicar, 'Miss Cleggy died by lightning: but we know that vengeance struck her down. I mention this point so you will know what to say at the inquest. You see, nobody would believe *this*.'

In those seconds I realized how right he was, realized what he had meant by saying the same power had put the file back on the shelf.

For there was no bell.

I turned stupidly, framed words. 'No — bell?'

'There has never been a bell,' the Vicar said. 'Where it really rings, or who rings it — No man knows.'

4

Invisible Murder

The vision of an ambulance hurtling through the London streets in the early evening, blasting a path by the savage clanging of its bell, is enough to stir almost anybody from preoccupation, and to a reporter like me it is a positive clarion call. I was just coming out of the doorway of the *London Argus* when the white vehicle swept by, took the danger traffic lights at full speed and carried on up the main road.

One thing registered automatically in my mind — a story — and even as I thought of it I had my own car engine roaring, whipped away from the curb, and raced with a supreme disregard for all law and order in the wake of the hurtling ambulance. As it was white I could follow it without difficulty under the high street lamps. I trailed it for four miles or so, out of the heart of the city to the lordly dignity of West Kensington. Finally the ambulance pulled up outside a residence in Kennedy's Crescent.

I jammed on my brakes, killed the ignition, then scrambled out of my car to join the ambulance men as they opened the rear of the vehicle and pulled forth a stretcher.

'What goes on?' I asked, and Tony, the ambulance driver whom I knew well, turned to me in surprise.

'You would be here,' he commented dryly. 'What do you do, smell these things out?'

'Official secret,' I told him.

'Well, I don't think there's much to interest you,' he said, heaving his end of the stretcher into his hands. 'It isn't a murder, and there's nothing lying around that even resembles a crime!'

I glanced back at the great shadowy house. For all the signs of life there were it might have been deserted for months. There was not even a glow behind the shades.

'Somebody phoned from here,' Tony

said, as I followed up the front path. 'Said he was dying — all alone — and to pick him up at once. Chap by the name of Dale Cavendish.'

I frowned, recalling something. We had found the front door open, and had stepped into the hall. It was here that it dawned on me where I'd heard the name before. Dale Cavendish! Of course! He had been scientific reporter on the *Daily Planet* about five years back.

No story? Well, I was beginning to feel interested, anyway.

I switched on the hall lights, and we three men glanced about us in mystification for a moment. There was nobody around. Then from somewhere down the corridor that led off the hall came a faint cry: 'Here . . . In here!'

Immediately we hurried along to a doorway through which high ceiling globes were casting a curious shadowless glow upon the room beyond.

'Gosh!' Tony exclaimed, 'What do you make of it?'

He said no more than this, since it was his job to attend to the man lying prone on the floor. He was not dead yet. He stirred flaccidly as the two ambulance men bent over him. I remained in the doorway, looking round a room which seemed to me to be an inchoate jumble of scientific apparatus, chiefly electromagnetic.

I'm not very much of a scientist, but I did recognize electromagnetic apparatus of a pretty advanced type, together with banks of insulators, complicated control boards, and in the midst of it all, seeming somehow like the central focus of the whole mass of junk, was an object like a gigantic enlarging camera depending from a girder athwart the ceiling, its narrowing end pointing towards the floor.

All this equipment sort of registered in my brain in a matter of seconds; my real attention was centred on the man on the floor, about whom the two ambulance men were now working. He was not very old, no more than thirty-three or four, and even if his face had not been contorted through the pain of some mysterious illness he'd developed he'd still have been mighty ugly. His nose was flat like a heavyweight's, and his lips thick and sensual. Only his forehead redeemed him. It was massive beyond the normal, with disordered dark hair, damp with the sweat of anguish, curling down it.

It was Dale Cavendish all right, I recognized that mop the moment I saw it — a bit older but still the face of the bad tempered bloke who'd been the scientific reporter of the *Daily Planet*, until he had quit to do scientific research.

'You'll — never get me to a hospital,' he whispered to Tony as he kneeled beside him. 'I telephoned and — and left the front door open just to — so's you could take that . . .'

He motioned weakly and closed his eyes for a moment. My gaze, and that of the ambulance men, moved to a machine rather like an outsized dictaphone standing on a bench. Like everything else in the place it was confoundedly complicated and possessed a multitude of wires leading back to the switchboards.

'It's — a — ' Dale Cavendish opened fading grey eyes for a moment. 'A — a thought — recorder. Everything's in it.

Don't move it. Just — just — ' He gulped for breath and twisted spasmodically. 'Just press the red button and — and let the power run. It'll — explain — '

He was silent for a while, and then whispered a few further words.

'He — managed it after all. Cleverer than I'd thought . . . '

That definitely was the last statement Dale Cavendish made. Though the ambulance men rushed him to hospital, he died on the way without further comments. So? Well, the police were informed and scientific apparatus not being in their line they asked Kensington Institute of Science to take a look round.

I don't know what they did or how they did it, but I do know that I was one of the reporters who heard the weird thought-recorder when it started explaining things. I'm hazy on the system it utilized, but the scientists who controlled it told us that thought vibrations had been imprisoned on sensitive vibration-reactive drums inside the thing, which in turn had been trans-formed into speech — or rather the words of the person who would have spoken had he been able. In a way it was like radio, only instead of electronic impulses being converted into sound, thought was converted instead, into easily understandable words.

That which follows is the story I noted down and which appeared condensed in the *Argus* because my editor didn't think the world in general was much interested in the doings of a rather obscure research scientist. My editor has no imagination, otherwise he'd have seen just how big an idea Dale Cavendish had really had.

See what you think . . .

* * *

My name is Robert Jesmond, and through the thought-recorder I am able to tell you the true facts leading up to the death, the murder if you like, of Dale Cavendish.

Cavendish and I first became acquainted through both of us happening to know Ellen Fielding. Though Ellen does not figure much in what I have to tell, I do think that she was the cause of all the trouble, albeit unconsciously. I met her first at a staff dance given by the Scientific Institute. My position was that of a physicist, of the lower grade. I loved my work, but it had a habit of worrying me. Still the pay was good and there was chance of promotion.

So when one of the boys in my department introduced me to Ellen I was irritated with myself to think that a red-haired, blue-eyed charmer of her type had been in the clerical department all the time and I'd never noticed.

'Bob Jesmond, eh?' she said, smiling and considering me under the bright lights as we sat together at the supper table after a pretty hectic evening. 'I believe I've seen you now and again, come to think of it.'

That was how it started off, and in an hour we were chatting as though we'd known each other all our lives. Then as we were leaving the building — I insisted on seeing her home — our walk amongst the merrymakers to my car on the parking ground was interrupted by a tall man in an overcoat and soft hat barring our path. I didn't know then who he was; all I did notice was that he was astonishingly ugly.

'Why, Dale, hello!' Ellen exclaimed, glancing up at him. 'So you managed to get along and meet me after all?'

'I said I'd see you home if I could spare the time, didn't I?'

He had a quiet yet peculiarly hard voice, as though he were keeping himself in check.

'Apparently I've wasted my time,' he added. 'You seem to be well taken care of.'

The grey eyes in the ugly face gleamed at me disapprovingly.

'Oh — er — Mr. Jesmond — Mr. Cavendish,' Ellen introduced us. 'Dale is a physicist, Bob, so you ought to have something in common.'

'Bob?' Dale Cavendish repeated. 'That sounds interesting. Been having a good time together?'

'Look here,' I said quietly. 'I don't particularly care who you are, Cavendish, but I don't like the way you behave! You — '

'Which of us is to see you home, Ellen?' he interrupted me.

'I — that is, we — ' Ellen looked from one to the other of us helplessly. I even thought I saw her beseeching me to go away.

'Apparently,' I said, looking at Cavendish, 'it has been your privilege up to now, and I wouldn't dream of upsetting it. Thanks for a happy evening, Ellen.' I smiled at her. 'I'll make a point of seeing you at the institute tomorrow.'

With that I left them to it, chiefly because there didn't seem to be anything else I could do — though I did wonder in a vague kind of way what a pretty girl like Ellen could see in an ugly devil like Dale Cavendish.

Next day I went out of my way to see her during the lunch hour and by degrees I got the facts out of her.

'I've known him quite a few months, Bob.' She smiled a little self-consciously. 'I met him when he used to be on the staff of the *Daily Planet* as science reporter. I had a job in the same office before I came here. We've sort of, well, gone about together. The only trouble is he's so moody; always thinking about scientific things. Half the time he forgets to keep his appointments, and that's why I can never rely on him — like last night, for instance. It was quite a surprise to me when he turned up.'

'Is there anything — serious in all this?' I asked.

She was silent; then she shrugged. 'He's wealthy, Bob. That means something.'

'He needs to be to offset a face like that,' I said bluntly, unable to keep it back.

'I suppose he is a bit clumsy featured,' she admitted. 'But he seems kind enough — except for last night when he blew up. I like him well enough.'

I considered her intently and finally she looked away and changed the subject. If I was to be good mannered I could not bring the matter up again, so I left it at that. But in private I made up my mind that I'd give Dale Cavendish a run for his money. I had taken a profound fancy to Ellen Fielding.

I was surprised, therefore, on returning to my apartment that evening to find Dale Cavendish awaiting me. The janitor had let him in and he was sprawled in an easy chair, smoking and glancing through a magazine. He got up the moment I entered and held out his hand. His big, ugly face was smiling.

'Hope you won't mind me barging in like this.' I shook his hand and considered him dubiously. 'I felt that I should apologize for last night. I didn't behave at all well. Just that I was a bit piqued. You know how it is sometimes.'

I murmured something and asked him if he'd have a drink. He accepted. We got to smoking, and by the end of an hour's chat I was quite convinced that he really was contrite. When he left it was with the invitation for me to call upon him and take a look at his scientific apparatus some time; as a scientist myself I might be interested.

I was interested, because I had heard a good deal at odd times about his scientific attainments. It occurred to me that I might learn plenty from a man of his talents. So a week later I called upon him and he showed me round his private laboratory.

It was the first of many calls on my part. In two months I was dropping in on him regularly, chiefly because I was by this time absorbed by some sort of theory he had on 'timeless evolution'.

'I see you don't grasp the idea, Bob,' he said one evening, when we were in his laboratory. 'To you evolution simply means progress through time, doesn't it?'

'Naturally. What else can it be?'

'That's natural evolution,' he said. 'There's another form of it — disorganization of energy.'

I contemplated the electromagnetic apparatus about us — particularly a gigantic instrument like an enlarging camera with a downwardly turned lens. Dale Cavendish stood regarding me with a faint smile on his abysmally ugly face.

'As we progress through time the more energy becomes disorganized,' he went on. 'You know the commonly accepted fact that there was more order in the universe yesterday than there is today.'

I nodded, and he spread his hands.

'Very well, then. If instead of waiting for normal progress to disorganize the atoms of which we're composed we artificially disorganize them, they can be made to form into a pattern they would normally possess at a much later date.'

'Presumably,' I said, 'the same effect as moving normally to the time when that pattern would exist?'

'Exactly!' He looked pleased. 'That's the purpose of this apparatus here.'

I studied the apparatus for a moment or two and then looked back at him. 'But look here, Dale, how do you know what sort of pattern future atomic setups will have? How can you plan for a fixed pattern produced by a given amount of disorganization?'

'I've spent years on that problem,' he answered, musing. 'Atoms, Bob, move in charted paths as the stars do. It is possible, by studying atomic science to the last detail, to predict with mathematical certainty what sort of a pattern will be produced from a given quantity of disorganization.

'That is, up to a point. If one tries to work it out too far, the accumulated postulations get out of hand. But, at least, I know what vibration is needed to produce a pattern of, say, a man as he will appear five thousand years from now!'

His eyes were upon me — piggy little grey eyes that had nothing in common with the brilliant brain he possessed.

'And after that?' I asked grimly.

He shrugged. 'I just don't know. There are limits to my calculations. Five thousand years' patterning is as far as I can get at the moment. It becomes conjecture after that, but obviously the patterns will form as they would have formed had normal evolution taken place. What comes after the man of five thousand years hence, I don't know. Not that I need to,' he added, and even then I didn't notice that a sinister edge had crept into his voice.

'But what's the good of the idea?' I demanded. 'What does it prove?'

'You're a scientist, and you ask me that! Isn't it obvious what a benefit it will be to scientific knowledge to know just how a

100

thing will be at a time in the future? With this system we can positively know the appearance of anything from a lump of soil to a man. Science can then plan and chart accordingly. That is what I propose to do, and incidentally make myself famous as the greatest mathematical scientist of my age . . . But there is a small personal matter to which I must attend first.'

I waited. He turned and to my surprise locked the door of the laboratory, then without glancing at me he went to the switchboard and closed several knife-blade contacts. I heard a hum of power from somewhere and the vibratory apparatus for the shuffling of atomic setups came to life. I watched the glowing tubes and complex meters with their quivering needles; then I moved my eyes to find Dale was studying me pensively.

'You're not a bad looking chap, Bob, are you?' he asked pensively.

I grinned. 'You don't expect me to answer truthfully, do you?'

'Compared to me, I mean.' He brooded. 'I'm as ugly as sin, and I know it. Ellen knows it too, but I think my other — er — attractions such as money, scientific fame, and so forth could have kept her interested in me — if you hadn't darned well got in the way!'

Suddenly his voice was hoarse, malignant. I stared at him in amazement. At that time I was, I suppose, pretty good looking — even handsome compared to Dale Cavendish — but naturally I had never taken it into account. It was only now, in this moment, that I saw how he really writhed at the thought of his own ugliness.

'I'm ugly, yes,' he breathed, clenching his fist and still glaring at me, 'but compared to a man of five thousand years hence I won't be! By present day standards a man that far ahead would be grotesque, a — a baroque!'

I glanced about me. Something ominous was coming. Jealousy had evidently gone to his head.

'Why do you think I've cultivated your friendship?' he demanded. 'Why do you think I have so lightly passed over your constant association with Ellen? For only one reason, to study you, to study your electronic pattern on my instruments without your being aware of it.

'I know all about you, Bob — and you're going to be my guinea pig! If you become a baroque — as you will! — I know Ellen won't have you. I don't say she will have me instead, but at least I'll stand a better chance than I do now.'

He broke off and nodded to an instrument rather like a radio beside the vibratory apparatus. 'See that?' he snapped.

'Well?' I asked coldly.

'It's a thought recorder. Your thoughts and mine are picked up by it and electronic processes convert them back into actual words so that everything that happens can be repeated. Even as you hurtle forward in a disorganization-path you will still think, and I shall know what you are thinking, and be able to turn the history of your scientific change to my own advantage.'

'The law will have something to say about that,' I told him grimly. 'Excluding the fact that I'm not quite the passive idiot you seem to imagine.'

He closed a switch and grinned crookedly. I said nothing but I felt some subtle, deadly influence sap every scrap of strength out of my system.

'Energy has been absorbed from you,' he said briefly. 'That magnetic instrument behind you is doing it. I can be sure of you this way. As for the law, I have that taken care of, too. You fell into the range of my instruments by accident. No witnesses can prove you didn't; none can prove you did. A man can't be convicted on those grounds in British law. You're going ahead five thousand years, my friend,' he whispered, approaching me, 'and before my eyes I'll watch you change, and know of what you are thinking!

'Five thousand years in about ten minutes. Interesting, isn't it? The vibrations of this apparatus of mine, mathematically planned, will shuffle your atomic setup into the pattern you would possess if by some fluke you could live five thousand years and evolve normally.'

I couldn't speak or move. I just stood and glared my helplessness; then suddenly he thrust out his hands and pushed me into the area of the thing like an enlarging camera lens. I landed flat on my back on metal plating, staring upwards at a glowing filigree of orange-tinted wires. They seemed to have a hypnotic effect upon me. I could feel my brain spinning in a gulf and the details of the laboratory became hazy.

Peculiarly enough I did not lose consciousness. I was still aware of who I was, but not of where I was. The orange glow above faded out after a while, and I was in a blank greyness in which nothing moved. It was odourless, tasteless, form-less, yet having a light that was neither sunshine nor daylight. Looking back on it I can only think that it must have been Time itself, so utterly jumbled and woven on itself that it made no sense. I was evolving, yes — if it could be called that. I was sternly conscious of the fact, but Time itself was a condition outside my development.

So, helpless in this blank gulf — for I could not rise from the metal plating, which, in fact, I could neither feel nor see — I lay staring at myself, along my body and then at my hands. With every passing second, if seconds they were, I was changing incredibly.

The shufflings and patternings that were going on electronically within me were more or less painless. There was instead a sense of tremendous inner movement, a feeling upon my skin as though the wings of butterflies were burring against it. I cannot describe it in any other way. But my limbs were narrowing in dimensions, my hands were losing their flesh and becoming like claws. Presently my clothes rotted and fell away from me. I knew why. Since they were included in the electronic dis-organization for 5,000 years ahead they naturally could not exist then, but I could, because the normal event of death did not enter into the calculation.

Presently my head began to ache, and I could tell that it was swelling. My eyes seemed capable of penetrating the mist a little.

Suddenly the opacity was gone and the laboratory had come back. The orange lights were right above me. The sense of helplessness left me, and with a still aching head I staggered, naked, to my feet.

Dale Cavendish was contemplating me from the switchboard, a look of profound awe on his blunted features.

'It's incredible!' he breathed, 'it's marvellous! I knew I couldn't be wrong.'

I passed my hands over myself, quickly. My body was far smaller than it had been. I was only about five feet high, balanced on pipestem legs and with the skinniest chest and hands imaginable. My head was the biggest thing about me, aching abominably and feeling terribly top heavy.

'Take a look at yourself,' Cavendish ordered grimly, and he nodded to a full-length mirror at the other end of the laboratory.

I stumbled to it and saw something with a mighty cranium, tiny socket-rimmed eyes, a buttonhole of a mouth. It was a distended, mad creature that moved when I moved. It was myself.

'Dale, you devil!' I swung round to him and then broke off, startled by the reediness of my voice.

'How do you feel, superman?' he asked dryly. 'Not that I need to ask you. Your thoughts were perfectly recorded and I know exactly what you experienced.'

His voice goaded me, and I hurled myself at him, but with the merest flick of his arm he sent me sprawling into a corner.

'Just as I'd expected,' he commented, brooding. 'Your atomic setup has configurated to that of a man five thousand years hence; and your brain-case has distended to allow for what, by normal evolution, would have been a superpowerful brain. Knowledge, however, is only gained through mental absorption in the normal course of time, therefore you have no more intelligence than you ever had despite the massive brain-case. The body has wasted at the expense of what would have been the mental — '

'How do you suppose you'll ever get away with this?' I shrieked at him, scrambling up again. 'You daren't reveal anything to the authorities because they'll know I was your subject!'

108

'I have no intention of revealing anything about you, Bob. I'm using you as a guinea pig, so that later on I can state my conclusions with absolute certainty, knowing that when a subject is chosen I can't help but be right because you will have gone before.' Cavendish paused, smiling cynically. 'If only Ellen could see you now!'

It was sheer blind, exasperated fury that hurled me at him, but as he had said, he was superstrong compared to me. I was flung back and once more tumbled into the area of that devilish electronic machine. The paralyzing effect began to work on me again, then Cavendish came forward and stood looking down at me.

'Obviously,' he said, 'I can't have you running around loose like this. That would be bad for me. And I'm also wondering what configurations lie beyond the five thousand year span. I can't compute them, but the apparatus will form the necessary patterns automatically. I think we ought to find out, don't you?

'You see, as I increasingly disorganize

the pattern of your atoms you become further and further removed from normal standards. And, by the way, the process is irreversible. There must finally come a time, I presume, when the limit is reached and you become a zero quantity with perfect thermodynamic equilibrium. Via the thought-recorder you can tell me what leads up to that state, can't you?'

Protest was useless, physical attack out of the question. He had the orange glow upon me again in a few seconds and once more the atomic shiftings overwhelmed me. The grey mist returned, and this time it seemed to last an interminable length of time. As on the previous occasion I did not lose consciousness, but became gradually aware of change stealing over me. The grotesque form was slowly but inevitably dissolving and becoming something else. I waited in a kind of horrified interest to discover what next I was to become.

I only began to receive the first clue when I noticed a change in my hands. They were altering into claws like those of a lobster! My legs too were extending into even thinner appendages, covered with fine hair. Extra legs were appearing from the region of the pelvis and at the same time my skin was giving place to a horny, shell-like substance.

How long it took for the metamorphosis to complete itself I have no conception. The one thing I did know was that I had lost the entity of man and had become a termite, of gigantic proportions. Cavendish must have been aware of what was happening from the thought-recorder, for when I merged back into the laboratory he was waiting for me with a gun levelled in his hand. Obviously my appearance gave him a shock; his expression showed it.

'I thought it might mean this, but I wasn't sure,' he said, staring at me. 'Amoeba, fish, ape, man, and then ant — to deal with the underworld life of earth as the surface cools. Yes, a biological necessity.'

Naturally I could not speak. Human speech had gone, but not human emotions. Something of Bob Jesmond still lived within me. I realized that I now had stupendous power, iron-hard mandibles with which to tear my tormentor to pieces.

Suddenly I sprang. Cavendish's revolver exploded but the bullet ricocheted off my shell-like exterior. I snapped my mandibles within an inch of his legs, but he twisted free just in time and snatched at a bottle of acid. Before he could grasp it my pincer claws had knocked his hand down and he went colliding into the bench.

He staggered away, whirled up a chair and smashed it futilely across my back. I went for him again, and then I got something I had not expected. He switched on the nozzle of the electric welding equipment and dived at me. My shell plating was not strong enough for that and I screeched involuntarily as the searing flame bit deeply into me.

Backwards I went, until too late I saw I was once again within the area of that orange glow. Holding me at bay with the flame Cavendish slammed switches with his free hand and plunged me into yet another utter disorganization of atomic paths. By degrees the termite I had been was changing yet again, and with the change the hurt of my burned body subsided.

What other form could there be beyond that of the termite? I was interested in wondering, in spite of being the victim. As far as I could imagine, the termite was the last stage of evolution. But I was wrong. Quite wrong.

All signs of a termite body disappeared. The claws, the appendages, the stalked eyes, the antennae. Instead I began to shrink with terrific speed and changed into something which, in comparison with normal standards, must have been — and still is — microscopically small. I wondered for a moment if the ultimate man was destined to descend into the microcosm to escape the rigours of a dead world. Then I grasped at the simple but astounding truth.

I had become a bacterium, a rod-like flagellum to be exact, and therefore endowed with the power of movement.

Dale Cavendish must have been aware of this also through the thought-recorder, but just the same he permitted me to come into the laboratory again. In fact I don't think he could help doing so, for I gathered that his apparatus only worked for a certain period, and then automatically stopped until a new pattern was set.

But this time I had Dale Cavendish where I wanted him!

As I returned to the laboratory I was beyond his visual range. He was a Colossus staring blankly at the apparently empty plate of the instrument. To me, the laboratory was gigantic and out of focus. Whether or not he had switched off the thought-recorder I don't know because the power of hearing had ceased for me. I don't think that I could really see either but in truth sensed everything by vibratory waves, an accomplishment that is normal to a lowly earthworm, and even more so to a bacterium.

I moved through the air of the laboratory as an invisible speck, and Cavendish, struggling to discover where I might be, made no effort to leave the laboratory. This suited me for I had the chance at last to strike back for the things he had done to me.

As I moved I realized why I had

become a bacterium. In the last stages of Earth's life, cold must grip it — a dead sun, a frozen world, all normal signs of life gone — except bacteria! Some forms of bacteria can survive and multiply in the zero of space and the torrid heat of boiling waters. In a word, the toughest form of life, the last to die, and the hardest to kill.

And here was I — sentient, with the knowledge of a man, consumed by only one thing, the longing for vengeance. At will I could become a saprophyte and do inestimable good for Dale Cavendish's constitution; or I could become a parasite and destroy him little by little. The choice was mine.

It was at this point, some time after I had merged back into the laboratory, that I think he must have switched on the thought-recorder to gain some idea of what I was thinking, for a dull resonant booming filled the laboratory. At my tiny size and working by vibratory senses only, the sounds didn't have any meaning for me. Not that I was much troubled. No matter what Cavendish learned of my thoughts he couldn't see me, and that was the point.

As I moved through the air I saw his gigantic face filling all the void. First I beheld intense interest, presumably as he listened to the reactions I had experienced in changing from a termite into a mobile bacterium; then gradually the look changed to one of deep fear as he realized I was somewhere in the laboratory, invisible, waiting for the chance to get at him.

Presently the booming noises ceased and he glanced anxiously about him.

I alighted gently on a crease of his laboratory smock and waited to see what he'd do next. He left the laboratory and went into the house. I was floating in the air near to him as he bathed himself thoroughly in disinfectant, presumably with the idea of making himself free from all taint of microbial dust.

It was amusing, and pretty futile! He had turned me into an invisible foe, and now he was desperately afraid of me. But at least he was scientist enough to know that I was beaten until he cut himself or

116

sustained some slight scratch, which would give me access to his bloodstream.

As it happened many days passed, and in this time he remained either in the house or in the laboratory, growing more and more confident as nothing happened to him. But from the thought-recorder he know that I was still hovering, waiting.

With everything being, to me, on such a vast scale I could not judge properly how he occupied his time in the laboratory, but it seemed that he was making endless notes on the villainous experiment he had carried out, and was evidently determined to cash in on the facts he had learned from me.

All this time he was careful to avoid causing himself injury, particularly when shaving, and I in the meantime had to sustain myself by consuming vegetable matter. Then one morning he made his mistake! In lifting a test-tube from its rack he caught it accidentally against the edge of the bench and the glass top splintered in his hand. Immediately blood welled.

His frantic efforts to disinfect the cut and swathe it rapidly in bandages were amusing to me. I hovered and still waited — for the blood to cease flowing. Then with my microscopic size I passed through the bandaging and torn flesh and became absorbed into his bloodstream. I became a parasite, a devouring, deadly parasite, breaking down healthy tissue at the fastest possible speed.

In an hour he knew he was doomed, though being within him I was not conscious of his actions. It was only when he began to cease moving that I emerged again from the selfsame cut by which I had entered. I found him lying on the floor with three men around him. I could not tell what they were saying but I was quite satisfied that Dale Cavendish was close to death.

I suppose the thought-recorder will reveal everything that has happened for I saw Cavendish motion towards it. What will happen to his invention I don't know, but possibly with all the facts laid bare by the thought-recorder it will be used by scientists with a less sadistic turn of mind for investigation into the mysteries of Time's future patternings.

As for me ... These are my last thoughts to be imprinted and played back over that machine. I have left behind me the world of Man, Superman, and Termite, and because of it have become emancipated. I can travel space, and to the stars themselves. I can plumb the deepest oceans and pass through the hottest fires.

I can go where I will, an indestructible bacterium, invisible to the eye of man, a dispenser of justice if I desire, or equally a giver of benefits.

I am that rare thing — a bacterium with the intellect of a modern man. In a way that compensates me a little for my lost birthright because, being a bacterium, I no longer have the emotions of man. Ellen, my laboratory job, the human pursuit of happiness, all gone, without regret. Dale Cavendish gave me one thing he never intended to give me — the key to the infinite.

5

From Afar

1

It is a remarkable story that I have to tell, but since I have the permission of the law, and of my wife to do so, I think that I ought to set the whole astounding experience on record since it is still occupying the energies of the world's greatest psychiatrists. Surely no married couple was ever so damned as Beryl and I from the start of our life together . . .

We were married on a glorious June day. Our engagement had not been a long one. In fact I had reached the age of thirty-seven, and had come to consider myself as almost a confirmed bachelor when a visit to a Birmingham stockbroker's firm brought me into contact with Beryl Wilson. At that time she was a very efficient secretary to a wealthy broker.

My own business being in stocks and shares I conceived all sorts of reasons for going to Birmingham, and finally — well, you know how such things are — Beryl Wilson became Mrs. Richard Shaw. I had become utterly entranced with this blonde-haired girl with the merry blue eyes. She was eight years my junior; filled with a terrible zest for living. I never knew a girl to love speed so much.

Taking it all round our marriage was a pretty quiet affair. When we left the church, we had already decided that our honeymoon would be spent at a quiet little hotel in Cornwall, to which I was going to drive us in my car. So, loaded up with luggage and with old shoes tied on the car's rear bumper we started off on that brilliantly sunny morning.

'Everything fixed?' Beryl asked me, when we were speeding down the country lanes.

'Everything,' I acknowledged smiling. 'I've arranged that we stop at the Ashdown Hotel for lunch, when we can also get rid of these fancy-dress clothes, then on again to Cornwall. We'll be there by teatime.'

'I suppose,' she mused, 'we are indeed absolutely alone — just together in the world if I can put it that way. You have only a housekeeper and a handyman; I have — or had — only a landlady. No parents — '

'And all the future before us,' I murmured. 'I'm fairly well off for money, with a good business. We don't need anybody to help us . . . '

Beryl nodded dreamily; then, as she watched the road ahead she sat up suddenly. Bright-eyed, she turned to me.

'Let me drive for a while, Dick, will you? You don't go half fast enough for my liking. You know how I like to get along — especially in a lovely roadster like this. Go on! Please!'

Well, it isn't easy to refuse your bride when she puts it like that; so I stopped the car and we changed places. I watched her slender, capable hands grip the steering wheel. She let in the clutch and depressed the accelerator gently — at first. For about a couple of miles she drove as sedately as if following a hearse, presumably to get the feel of the car, then her merry blue eyes glanced at me.

'Feel in the mood for a nice, swift run?' she asked me, impishly.

'Within limits,' I responded, a trifle uneasy as I remembered her weakness.

My assent settled it for her. Gradually her foot pressed lower on the accelerator, and I watched the speed indicator creep up from forty to fifty, then gradually, to sixty. We were in an unrestricted area, of course, with a straight sunlit lane devoid of traffic ahead of us, but even so it seemed a pretty alarming rate to me.

But Beryl was not nearly satisfied yet. She was enjoying every moment of this, the wind blowing the blonde hair back from her lovely face, her eyes fixed keenly straight ahead. Sixty — sixty-six — seventy — seventy-five — !

'Berry!' I cried at last. 'Berry, for heaven's sake ease up a bit!'

'Why? We're only just getting a real move on — !' And she added five miles an hour to the speed in mischievous retaliation. Then, suddenly, it happened! I could not be quite sure what occurred but I noticed a queer expression settle on

Beryl's face. It was not the look of sudden illness but more of fear and intense perplexity.

This seemed odd to me for I had never seen her afraid in all the time I had known her, and certainly never perplexed. Perhaps it lasted fifteen seconds, then, quite abruptly, her features went blank and her hands dropped from the wheel into her lap.

'Beryl — !' I screamed, but it was too late then.

Going at its present speed and uncontrolled, the car lost the crown of the road and hurtled straight for the bank. For a numbing split second I saw a telegraph pole hurtling towards me.

The rest was an exploding, tearing hell of steel, glass and leather. Then —

Darkness.

★   ★   ★

My mind is in complete confusion concerning the events that followed the smash. I have a dim remembrance of chaotic dreams, of visions of nurses going to and fro, and once the outlines of an operating theater pervaded my consciousness . . . Until at last I became rational enough to be able to understand where I was, and ask questions.

Sealed in a plaster cast from waist to shoulders I learned that I had sustained several broken ribs, a fractured arm, and multiple cuts and abrasions. But now it was only a matter of convalescence.

'And my wife?' I asked the doctor in charge of my case. He did not answer immediately.

'I want the truth,' I went on quickly. 'Why don't you answer my question?'

He looked at me steadily and I felt the grip of horror.

'Doc, you don't mean that she's — she's dead?'

'No, not dead,' he reassured me. 'She sustained multiple injuries from the crash just as you did, but we've fixed her up all right. As far as we can tell medically she is a normal woman again, except for one thing — the way she looks at you.'

'The — the way she *looks* at you?' I repeated in astonishment.

'I don't think I have ever seen such a strange light in the eyes of a woman before! It's mysterious — eerie, yet somehow contemptuous. Her face though remains expressionless. All the pain she has endured has not even made her wince! Yet her nervous system is not in any way injured. I'm afraid I can't explain it to you very well. You will have to see her for yourself — when you're better — '

With this he left me, and of course, from then onwards my one anxiety was to get well again and find out what had happened to my beloved Beryl. Even so it was another six weeks before my wish was gratified and by this time she too was ready for discharge. So, for the first time since the accident we met each other in Dr. Mason's office.

Now I realized what Mason had meant. To all outward appearances my wife was as young and good to look at as ever, trimly smart in the costume that had been provided for her, but there *was* a difference, an intense paleness of face, explainable perhaps by the ordeal she had been through; and those eyes! How changed they were indeed — *how* changed!

Certainly she looked at me in full recognition, but with such indefinable insolence that my intended greeting died without being uttered. Instead I felt an uncommonly strong desire to hit her. I cannot describe what else I saw in her eyes; they were depthless, mysterious, had the peculiar quality of looking at me and yet at the same time beyond me to . . . somewhere.

'You are Richard Shaw, my husband, aren't you?' she asked me in level tones.

I stared at her. 'Well of course I am!' I answered in amazement. 'Of all the extraordinary questions!'

She shrugged her shoulders.

'Since we have been parted from each other so long I thought it as well to make sure.'

Just for a moment I wondered if this was one of her mischievous tricks, then her utterly impassive expression convinced me otherwise. She had meant every word in all seriousness.

'I believe,' Dr. Mason said, glancing at her, then at me, 'that Mrs. Shaw is still suffering from the effects of the accident — '

'Nothing of the kind!' Beryl interrupted. 'You made a thorough examination of me this morning and pronounced me quite fit to be discharged. You must remember it.'

'Yes,' Mason admitted. 'That is true.'

He looked at her for a moment as though trying to make up his mind about something, then he turned back to me again. 'In accordance with your wishes, Mr. Shaw, I have had all the necessary arrangements made. Your car — repaired now I understand — is in the Crossways Garage. I had your home contacted and your housekeeper is expecting you and Mrs. Shaw today. A taxi will be here shortly at three o'clock. In fact,' Mason added, glancing through the window, 'I believe it is here now.'

He got to his feet and pressed a button. A porter came and took away the bags, retrieved from the car, then Beryl looked at me expectantly and rose from her chair. Without so much as a word of farewell or thanks to Mason she followed the porter from the room. It was so unlike her usual graciousness I just couldn't understand it.

'I must apologize for her, Doctor,' I said worriedly. 'I've no idea why she is behaving like this. She seems to have forgotten everyday manners.'

'And yet she reacted perfectly to every psychological test we gave her. So it isn't a peculiar form of amnesia . . . ' Mason's craggy face became thoughtful for a moment; then finally he shrugged. 'She's the queerest patient I have ever known.'

I shook the big hand he held out to me and he saw me to the door. Beryl was seated in the back of the taxi, waiting for me.

'He wants to know where we're going,' she said, nodding to the driver. 'Since I don't know you'd better tell him.'

'But, Berry, you know where my home is: you've been to it many a time. What-ever's the matter with your memory?'

'Suppose you tell him where to go and stop bothering about my memory?'

I hesitated for a moment, then turned to the driver:

'Keep on going until you get to the village, then I'll direct you from there.'

He nodded and closed the door upon us when I had settled beside Beryl. Soon we were speeding down the Sanatorium driveway and so out into the main road.

We had covered five miles and gone right past that fateful spot where we had had the collision before Beryl seemed to think it necessary to speak again, and then her words only served to deepen the confusion in my mind.

'What are we going to do with our lives from now on, Richard Shaw?'

'Did — did you call me — Richard Shaw?' I whispered.

'Yes, of course. That's your name, isn't it?'

I caught at her hand and held it tightly.

'Listen, Berry, if this is some kind of a joke you are trying to keep up for God's sake bring it to an end right now. I've had every bit as much as I can stand! Richard Shaw indeed! I'm Dick to you, and always have been, just as you are Berry to me.'

The absurdity of having to explain such a thing to her did not occur to me at the moment. Actually I think I believed at that time that she definitely was a victim of some kind of brain trouble. And yet she did not look vague — anything but it. Her blue eyes were fixed on me, gazing, not exactly at me, but through me, to something beyond . . .

'All right,' she said presently, 'it's Dick from now on. But I still want to know what we are going to do with our lives. What does one usually do?'

This was about the limit! I was beginning to think of myself as a teacher forced to instruct a grown woman with the brain of a child. What a task for a newly-married husband who had been looking forward to wedded bliss!

'You really mean you don't know — or at any rate can't remember — how we are to live?' I asked incredulously.

'I mean just that, yes. Why do you take so long to answer?'

'Because it's such a damned impossible thing to realize!' I retorted. 'Anyway we are going to live together 'until death us do part,' else we run into such intolerable circumstances that we decide to part legally from each other.'

'I understand we are going to live in your house?' she asked after a while.

'Right,' I assented. 'You'll soon get your health back there. There will be plenty of people about to keep you from getting depressed — '

'I don't like people,' she interrupted. 'In fact I don't think your home is going to suit me for a moment. I want somewhere quiet and undisturbed, where the only interruptions are those we make ourselves.'

'You want quiet!' I exclaimed. 'Berry, to me you just aren't the same girl. Why, until the accident your one joy in life was the company of other people. You just lived on thrills, went the round of the shows. This new attitude is beyond my understanding.'

'Don't forget that I've been ill,' she said — but I felt somehow that she was only using this for an excuse. 'It's only natural that I should want rest and quiet — '

She broke off and pointed suddenly through the window.

'There! That's the kind of place I mean!'

I looked quickly as the taxi went

speeding along the main road, and for a moment I had a glimpse of a massive, detached house, extremely old-fashioned in the Georgian style, lying well back in its own grounds. Slanting lopsidedly over the untidy hedge was a notice board 'FOR SALE,' but we were going too fast for me to get the name of the agent.

'That would be marvelous!' Beryl breathed, looking back through the rear window. 'So quiet . . . so restful!'

She swung round to me with the first show of emotion she had revealed so far.

'Dick, I want that place!' she said abruptly.

'We'll talk about it later,' I promised, but all the same I made up my mind that I wouldn't even refer to it again unless she did. Its very appearance had given me the creeps . . .

She became silent again, but I noticed that she paid particular attention to the name of the village as we passed an Automobile Club sign — Bilton-on-Maybury. Evidently she had conceived a liking for the place even if I hadn't.

Very little further conversation passed

between us until twenty minutes later the taxi drew up outside my home. I helped Beryl to alight while the driver went ahead with our bags.

Beryl stood surveying the house for a time, then she looked at the busy main road, and sighed.

'We're not going to stay here, Dick!' Her voice was so cold and decisive on this point it did not even leave me the chance to argue.

Mrs. Wilson, my cheery old house-keeper, was there at the door to welcome us. She directed the taxi driver to put the bags in the hall, then turned to us with a smile. Beryl, though, gave her one look and strode right past her to finish up in the middle of the hall looking about her. Mrs. Wilson looked after her with a curious, rather hurt gaze, then she turned back to me.

'Glad to see you back again, Mr. Shaw,' she said, in genuine pleasure. 'What a terrible thing it was to happen to you and — and Mrs. Shaw! And just as you were going on your honeymoon, too!'

'We're all right now,' I assured her.

Then, bethinking myself I added rather dubiously, 'At least I am. I'm afraid Beryl is still suffering from the after-effects . . . I want you to meet her. Berry!' I called.

Lost in thought Beryl gave a noticeable start, then she came forward slowly.

'Berry, I want you to meet our housekeeper, Mrs. Wilson. She and her husband take care of everything — '

'He's out shopping,' Mrs. Wilson added, her eyes fixed in a kind of bewilderment on Beryl's face.

'You mean,' Beryl said, looking at me, 'that this is one of our servants?'

'Well, not exactly that.' For I had seen Mrs. Wilson stiffen indignantly.

'In my bachelor days Mr. and Mrs. Wilson were pretty nearly father and mother to me.'

Beryl pondered this for a moment, then she looked at Mrs. Wilson steadily.

'My husband may have sentimental attachment towards you, Mrs. Wilson — and towards Mr. Wilson — but as far as I am concerned you are still a servant. You will oblige me by remembering it

. . . Now what about a meal? I am feeling very hungry.'

'I have it ready in the dining room,' Mrs. Wilson replied curtly. 'By the time you have both freshened up I will be ready to serve it.'

Off she went to the kitchen, positively bristling. I picked up the bags and led the way upstairs with Beryl following slowly behind me, looking about her at the same time. When she came into the bedroom I gave her a grim look.

'Beryl, your attitude's intolerable!' I snapped. 'If Mrs. Wilson and her husband stay on after this I'll be surprised!'

She took off her hat and straightened her hair before the dressing-table mirror.

'I am not in the least concerned what they do. But I shall continue to treat that woman — and her husband when I see him — for what they are — servants!'

2

There it was. I have tried to make clear the extraordinary start to my married life and the incredible metamorphosis of Beryl, but as yet I was only at the beginning of the revelations concerning her.

Not having dined with her since before our accident I had had no opportunity to see how she behaved at a meal; and what I did behold made me wonder what on earth they must have thought of her at the Sanatorium . . . Imagine my amazement when she handled her knife and fork with extreme awkwardness, and at first even in the wrong hands!

I watched her actions with a deep, worried interest, trying — as I had been trying all along — to imagine what had so changed the girl I had married. When finally she got the knife and fork to her liking, holding them rather like chop-sticks, she looked across at me with a most extraordinary look in her eyes. It was as though she had guessed I was going to ask questions and was determined to forestall me.

Under the impact of those strange and abysmal eyes of hers all thoughts of interrogating her went out of my mind. At the time I did not know why, but then I did not comprehend even the vaguest outlines of the incredible thing that had happened.

Mrs. Wilson, after her first umbrage, had now drifted into utter bewilderment, and I gathered she had had a few lurid things to say to her husband, too. By now she sensed as keenly as I did that there was something very peculiar about my wife. For this very reason — her curiosity — I hoped that she and her husband would stay on. Unless, of course, Beryl drove them out.

Then suddenly, in the midst of the meal, Beryl asked a question: 'Dick, how much do you know about that village of Bilton-on-Maybury?'

'Nothing,' I answered, 'except that it is obviously a dead-alive hole.'

'By that I suppose you mean that there is nobody to bother about save a few stupid villagers?'

I realized that I had quite unintentionally played into her hands. Tightening my lips I waited for what she was going to say next. It came soon enough.

'Tomorrow we're going to live in that house we saw!'

'As easily as that, eh?' I asked. 'Just walk in, live there, and forget everything else?'

Just for a moment she looked puzzled.

'Well, why can't we?' she demanded.

'Because — ' I threw down my napkin impatiently. 'Listen, Berry, it's time you and I got a few things straight! I can't believe that your brain has been so affected by that smash that you've even forgotten normal everyday procedure. If this attitude of yours is a joke, for God's sake stop it! I've had as much as I can stand!'

'I simply asked you why we can't go and live in that house, that's all!' Her voice was cold, and yet surprised. 'Explain why. It's empty, isn't it?'

'Agents! Money to purchase! Deeds to be signed!' I was nearly shouting at her. 'All those things have to be done.'

'Oh!' She nodded slowly, then she gave a shrug. 'Well, what's to stop us doing it? The trouble with you, Dick, is that you are always raising so many difficulties when something has to be done.'

'I'm not sure yet that it's going to be!' I retorted. 'There is not the slightest reason why we should give up this house here, within easy reach of the city, to go and live in a dump like that. Do you realize that it would mean a thirty-mile trip for me every day? And judging from the remoteness of the railway station I'd have to use my car. The expense wouldn't be worth it.'

'Oh, but it would!' she said, then, as I looked at her in astonishment she added slowly, 'I think there is something you ought to know. I intend to get what I want and you can't raise a finger to stop me. If you try to, you may get a shock!'

I gave a cynical, disbelieving smile, and it seemed to infuriate her.

'Fill that tumbler with water!' she ordered, pointing to it beside my elbow. 'Then drink it off without a pause!'

Don't ask me why, but I did just that. To my mind, at that moment, there was nothing in the world so important as her command. So, though I was not thirsty, and despite the fact that the tumbler was a big one, I drained it to the last drop. Even as I set it down I gasped a little for breath. Realizing what I had done I gazed at her fixedly, but for some reason I had to look away again. There was an unearthly, dominant fire in those eyes of hers.

'Hypnotism!' I whispered. 'That was it, wasn't it? You made me do that!'

She did not answer. In fact she had no need to do so for I knew it was the truth. Then, suddenly, she got to her feet and went over to the window. The twilight was closing in and stars were gleaming vaguely in the misty blue sky.

It struck me as I watched her that for just a moment there was an expression of deep longing on her pale, unemotional face. She muttered something, half to herself, but I caught one word —

' — *Andura!*'

Then, as though she had completely forgotten my presence, she turned and left the room.

★ ★ ★

For reasons best known to herself, but decidedly unwifely from my point of view, Beryl elected to sleep in a room by herself, so I had no opportunity to question her further . . . The following morning she was at breakfast, as cold and aloof as ever.

'We are going to see about that house, of course?'

It was not a question but an order, and though I had made up my mind beforehand that I was going into the city to catch up on my neglected business I now had not the nerve to say so — not with those eyes of hers fixed upon me.

'Yes, we'll go,' I assented, 'but I still think it is very foolish.'

'What you think, Dick, does not interest me in the least!'

I looked at her bitterly and went on with my breakfast, then as soon as it was over we left the house and took the 'bus for Bilton-on-Maybury. I had not picked up my repaired car as yet, of course, and after what had happened I wasn't particularly anxious to get it, either.

The 'bus stop was only ten minutes'

walk away from the empty house, so we had plenty of chance to study it as we approached. I have said already that from the taxi it had looked a dreary hole. Seen now in the bright morning sunshine it showed up in all its leprous unpleasantness.

Its outer walls, as we saw them from the tree-lined drive, were badly weather-stained, and in some places the eaves were coming away from their supports. Added to this dismal aspect were the many dirty windows, the cracked front door, and the general air of untidiness hanging about the neglected grounds.

For my part, I made up my mind in a few minutes about the place, but Beryl reacted in a totally different way. For some reason it all fascinated her. She went back and forth, peering in at the windows, studying the gratings that proclaimed basements, looking at the hot, tangled grounds.

'We don't need anybody to come and let us in here,' she said finally. 'We can get in for ourselves. Here, smash this window!'

'But, Berry, I can't do that! I just can't go about smashing up other people's property — '

'It'll be our property soon enough,' she interrupted. 'Go on! Smash it! Nobody can see you from the road.'

I hesitated for a moment, then picking up a stone I hurled it through the pane she had indicated. Smashing away the remaining sharp pieces I clambered through the broken window into an old-fashioned dungeon-like kitchen. I was just about to go to the front door and let Beryl in when to my surprise she came scrambling through the window.

I never saw such eager interest on anybody's face. She paid no attention to me: her whole energy was given to examining the place. I followed her from room to room, and presently up a massive staircase to the bedrooms. Every window looked out on to open countryside. The only other habitations visible were a cluster of cottages and small-time shops that made up the village of Bilton itself, and a yellow brick, old-fashioned residence in its own grounds, perhaps two miles away.

For a long time Beryl studied the view as though pondering something, then off she went again on her survey. We finished up in the huge, rambling basement which I judged had been used as a wine cellar by the previous occupier.

'Well?' I asked finally, striking my umpteenth match down in this cold, dank place. 'What do we do now?'

'Do!' Beryl echoed. 'As if there could be any doubt! We are going to live here!'

'Oh, we are? Suppose it is more than I can afford?'

'No such contingency has got to enter into it!' she retorted. 'It's ideal for my purpose. The very place I've been looking for. And I've got to have it.'

I looked at her in the flickering match-light for a moment, then, taking her arm, I led her upstairs and into the lounge.

'Beryl,' I said bluntly, 'you said something down there which needs explaining — something about this ancient dump being just right for your purpose. *What* purpose?'

'That doesn't signify and you wouldn't

understand it anyway. All you have got to do is buy this place right away.'

There it was, and though I daresay you are by now thinking me a pretty spineless specimen, I obeyed her wishes to the letter because there was nothing else I could do. Back of my mind was the memory of that glass of water the previous night. It was only water that time, but the next . . . ?

We were at the Agent's in half-an-hour, and within another half hour I was in possession of a temporary property transfer until the actual conveyance should come along. But I was also very much lighter in the bank, which did not please me at all. In fact the only satisfaction I got out of the business was that Beryl looked really happy for the first time since she had left the Sanatorium.

3

I had plenty on my plate for the next fortnight. Beryl's mind seemed to be a complete blank on everything except what she *wanted*. The means of getting it never seemed to occur to her. Rather she seemed to think she could *take* whatever she needed, and the increasingly evident fact that she could not made her impatient. I had all my work cut out steering her clear of pure and simple kleptomania.

Otherwise I did all she asked. Got the place furnished as she wanted it, and had the big and ancient sign 'The Beeches' put up properly outside the gates, installed Mrs. Wilson and her husband. Yes, I even traveled in my own car thirty miles to business every day, not forgetting the thirty miles back, and all the time I wondered what in hell for.

How Beryl occupied her time while I was away I had no idea of course, but from her reserved comments and those of the servants I gathered she spent a lot of time shopping — and going to London on the local 'bus service to do it! Now why should she — ?

Definitely, I was getting all tied up. And her attitude was most unhelpful when after a week of this sort of thing, I tackled her directly about it.

'Why should it concern you, Dick?' she

asked tonelessly, as we sat at dinner in the dining hall in the gloom of the fall evening. 'I don't ask you what you do in your office. Why does it matter what I do here?'

'That isn't like you, Berry,' I said reproachfully. 'Before the car smash we shared all our joys and sorrows at the end of the day, but now — I don't understand you! Hang it, it's almost as though you're not the same girl!'

'Is it?' She went on eating, unmoved. I put a blunt question.

'What have you been buying in town, anyway?'

'Books — instruments — odds and ends. I feel the need of a hobby.'

I frowned. 'What sort of books? I filled nearly a library full in this place — '

'But you did not include up-to-date directories. I bought one or two. Thought I'd like to study up on a few people. *Who's Who* stuff.'

I opened my mouth to comment, but I just could not. It was too much for me. Besides, I couldn't see any books, or instruments, or odds and ends . . .

'They're in the basement,' Beryl said, as though she had read my thoughts. 'Only I'd rather you didn't go down there. I've got a sort of den and you might upset things.'

I flung down my knife and fork and exploded: 'Look here, what sort of a damned set-up is this — ?'

I had to stop short because Mrs. Wilson came in. She started to say something about an Inspector, then a big man with woolly white hair, a red face, and shrewd gray eyes came in behind her. He had on a heavy overcoat and held his hat in his hand.

''Evenin' folks! Sorry to butt in like this ... Inspector Hilton's the name — law an' order in this little community. I'd like a few words with you.'

I recovered suddenly from my surprise. 'Why — er — sure. Take a seat, won't you?' Then I dismissed Mrs. Wilson and introduced Beryl. Hilton nodded, then his red face became grim.

'It's a matter o' murder,' he said. 'Over at the 'Mount'. I'm handling it until the Yard takes over. So, I thought I'd make a few inquiries ... You may know that Boyd Harkness, the retired millionaire candy king, lived at the 'Mount'.'

I remembered that the residence was about two miles away.

'I've heard so,' I nodded. 'Murdered, eh? That's bad.'

'Yes. Strangled.' Hilton's tiny little gray eyes flashed from me to Beryl. 'Strangled, with a piece of cord wrapped three times round his neck,' he added slowly.

We waited, then he said, 'You're new around here, eh?'

'Meaning — what?' I asked him shortly.

'Nothin' — 'cept that you're new. The crime up at the 'Mount' is a blunderer's job. Footprints all over the grounds outside the room where Harkness was found. We know a possible culprit already: a homicidal maniac escaped from the Larchwood Mental Hospital this mornin' — and it may be him. *May* be, I said. Looks as though it might be a maniac because there's no rhyme nor reason to the murder. No stealin' — unless you'd call the theft of a paperweight stealin' ... '

'A paperweight?' I repeated. 'That's odd.'

150

'Yes. A maniac, as I said — and that's why I'm here. Seen anybody unusual knockin' around here today? Nobody unusual called?'

'I've been away all day,' I told him. 'You seen anybody, Berry?'

'Nobody.'

Her voice was completely final and her eyes looked at Hilton steadily. He looked back at her, ran his finger along his jaw. He cocked an eyebrow.

'Either of you know Harkness?' he asked abruptly.

'We have never seen the man,' Beryl stated.

'Right enough,' I confirmed. 'Only heard of him by hearsay . . . But look, Inspector, why are you so sure it *was* murder? Couldn't it have been suicide?'

'No. There was a loaded revolver in the desk drawer right beside the body. Do you think a man would wrap and knot cord round his neck, die in that painful way, if he could have put a bullet through his brain in quarter the time? I don't . . . '

He got to his feet. 'Paperweight's the queerest thing,' he mused, then with another look at Beryl's impersonal calmness, he gave a shrug. 'Well, thanks a lot for everythin'. I'll be on my way.'

'You won't have a drink or something?' I asked him.

'No, no — not while I'm on duty . . . '
He nodded and went off. Mrs. Wilson saw him out. Once the front door had closed I lay back in my chair, frowning. Beryl gave me that look that went through me, through the wall, out beyond — Somewhere . . .

4

'Queer!' I summed up finally. 'Very queer!'

'I suppose it is,' Beryl acknowledged, proceeding with her interrupted meal.

'Satisfies me on one thing,' I said firmly. 'I'm taking a vacation from the office. Can't leave you around here while there is a maniac on the run. I'd never have an easy moment.'

'You don't have to worry about me, Dick. You attend to your business. I'm quite safe. Quite!'

'But you can't be sure of that!' I protested.

'Yes I can. You see . . . that accident did something to me, something you have never known about.' Beryl paused. 'I cannot be hurt,' she finished.

You cannot imagine the way she said that. It was ghoulish — eerie. And as I stared at her amazedly she suddenly turned her knife blade over and drew it casually across her palm. Instantly blood welled from the thin, deep cut. And she watched it, dispassionately, not batting an eyelash!

Immediately I was on my feet, dashed round to her and wrapped my handkerchief round the wound. She gave the faintest of cold smiles at my horror.

'Why do you look so frightened, Dick?' she asked quietly. 'I felt no pain at the injuries I got from the car smash; I feel no pain from anything. What *is* pain I wonder? A mental state — ?'

'Berry, in God's name stop saying such ghastly things!' I cried hoarsely. 'For pity's sake, what's come over you? What's *wrong*?'

She tightened the handkerchief slightly, but the matter of her incredible act seemed to have gone right out of her mind.

'So you'll not take a vacation from your office?' she asked slowly; then as I did not answer she turned to look at me and repeated her words, only now it was not a question but a statement.

For me the room was suddenly nothing but two blue eyes — unwavering blue eyes in which the pupils seemed unusually dilated. In them I seemed to see deep glowing pools of fire. I felt stirred by an inexplicable command. Curious, but all of a sudden I was wondering why I had ever even thought of staying at home anyway.

'No, I won't take a vacation,' I said finally; then I went back rather unsteadily to my chair, monkeyed around with the rest of my meal, then gave it up as a bad job. I had a headache too.

I got up again uneasily. Beryl's eyes followed me as I went to the fireplace and dragged out my pipe. By this time my brain was a cauldron of doubts, suspicions, perplexities . . . If only I could figure out what was wrong with her!

I fumbled for my matches for my pipe: I had none. A log fire burned in the old-fashioned grate. I dived my hand into the ornamental waste-basket beside it and pulled out a chunk of crumpled brown paper. I started to make a taper — Then I stopped in amazement! All else forgotten I smoothed the crumples out of the paper and stared at an adhesive label upon it. A name and address — *Beryl's* name!

This address! The village postmark!

Then Beryl came up to me. She took the paper, tore off an end, threw the rest in the fire. She held the paper taper for me and I drew the flame mechanically through my tobacco. My eyes met hers over the smoky, dancing flame.

'Who'd be sending you parcels locally?' I demanded roughly.

She threw the taper away and did not reply. Savagely I pressed the bell button. Mrs. Wilson came. From her I learned the parcel had come by the afternoon mail.

'Okay,' I said, scowling. 'That's all . . . '

'Well?' Beryl enquired, as I chewed my pipe savagely.

'There's only one place in this darned backwater where a parcel like this could come from,' I said grimly. ' 'The Mount'! Our place and the 'Mount' are the only two houses in the district, and you certainly would not have anything sent up from that petty-fogging village — not with London as your shopping centre — Berry, it's time for a showdown! What do you know about that parcel? More — what do you know about the murder of Boyd Harkness?'

'I have never even met Harkness,' she answered steadily. 'And you are allowing yourself to jump to idiotic conclusions — '

'Idiotic be damned! Haven't you given me enough cause to worry recently? Acting like an — an automaton, gazing at things in that blood-curdling way . . . I'm going to find out what's wrong with you, Berry, even if it kills me!'

'Hadn't you better make quite sure that it doesn't?' she asked, then as I gave her a puzzled look she turned away. 'I have my hobby to attend to,' she added from the door. 'I'm going down into the basement, and if you want good advice don't follow me. My hobby is rather a dangerous one, and you might get hurt!'

'And you think I'll sit here and let you — ?'

'I *know* you will!'

She still looked at me from the door. Once more I had that conviction that the room was nothing but her eyes. As though impelled by an invisible hand I moved from the fireplace and sank into the armchair, gazing at the flames in the fire.

Yes, I heard the door click behind her. I heard the half-hour and then the hour strike from the hall clock, but I remained where I was, watching patterns in the crumbling red-hot logs.

When I forced myself back to effort my pipe was dead ashes, and Beryl was before me again in the flickering glow. Twilight had died into night.

The ghost of a thin, cold smile hung round Beryl's lips.

'I think,' she said, 'it is time to retire . . . '

My fitful sleep was tormented by the wildest nightmares. Inspector Hilton,

Beryl's eyes, a knife blade, brown paper, and lengths of cord knotted three times round a neck were all mixed up, and through the midst of it danced a massive object that had served as a paperweight for a dead candy king!

Mad! Chaotic! It left me dull and heavy next morning, but there was still no thought in my mind of staying behind to look after Beryl in case that maniac — No, hang it! The very thought had been killed in my brain. But why? Was it feasible that Beryl had killed it? If so — How?

She was as calmly inscrutable as ever during breakfast: her hand had healed a good deal too. I left her brusquely, did not even trouble to kiss her as I had on previous mornings. Since the showdown of the previous evening there seemed to radiate from her an alien coldness. It was not so much a material thing as a mental one. Between Beryl, the girl I had loved and married, and this impersonal white-faced, frozen-voiced woman there was a gulf, an unexplainable barrier through which I just couldn't penetrate — yet.

In London though, freed from the dreary shackles of the house, I emerged somewhat from the depths and did plenty of hard thinking. She had mentioned *Who's Who*. Well, maybe something in that. I had the current edition brought to me and, as I had hoped, Boyd Harkness' name was given in full, together with his achievements.

Most of it was praise for his climb from newspapers to commercial eminence as the candy king, but towards the end of the eulogy was a section that impressed me a lot. It read:

' — and amongst the many souvenirs of his private collection of antiques may be mentioned a part of the famous 'Bloodstone', of which there are only three others in the world. Valueless as gems, they are nevertheless unique for their antiquity, having been handed down from time immemorial — '

Bloodstone? Never heard of it! But I had heard of a paperweight that the thing might have become, since it possessed no value outside of its antiquity.

That struck me as an angle, so after

lunch I browsed through the public library, and in *Gems, Stones and their Origins* I hit on the Bloodstone at last. The writer said:

'A species of mineral allied to the carbon group, but remarkable for its deep blood-red hue. Originally the bloodstone was one massive piece of glasslike mineral, and was found in a remote corner of Arkansas by a trader in 1548. It was then handed down through various families. In 1630 it was split into four parts and became a prize for antique hunters. The four sections in the present day are owned by, Mr. Boyd Harkness, of Bilton-on-Maybury, Essex; Mr. Henry Carson, of Mayfair, London, a famous sportsman; Madame Elva Borini, the celebrated Italian primadonna, of Naples, Italy; and Dr. Kenneth Cardew, resident attaché to the British Embassy in Bermuda.

'The actual origin of the stone is lost in antiquity. Science has puzzled over the fact that it represents no mineral form known on earth; therefore it seems not illogical to assume that perhaps it came in the dim past from a passing meteor, or as the result of some fusion in the cosmos — '

Yes, definitely I had got something! Though it did not by any means explain Beryl's queer behavior. I realized that before me there lay a trial such as a detective is usually called upon to take; and, like a detective, I realized that a slip-up on my part might mean an untimely end. Beryl had warned me of that, and I was more than sure that she was not joking . . .

* * *

I left the office early and called on Inspector Hilton on my way home.

'How'd you make out at the 'Mount'?' I asked him.

He shrugged. For some reason his manner seemed evasive.

'Not so well. We caught the maniac anyway — or rather the Asylum people did. He was twenty miles away from the 'Mount' when they got him, a distance far too great for him to have been connected with the murder of Harkness. At the moment it's a case of murder by a person

161

or persons unknown — '

I nodded slowly, then reminded him he had said something about footprints.

'The gardener's,' he said. 'Last night when I called up at your place I hadn't got all the facts. I have now.'

There was something about the way he looked at me with his keen little gray eyes, something about the calm evasiveness of his manner —

'Have you any ideas?' he asked quietly. 'Is that why you came?'

I bluffed my way out of this. 'No. Just that your call last night has got me interested in the business — Harkness being our nearest neighbor, I mean. I'm glad you got the maniac, though. It's a load off my mind.'

'I'm glad,' he said, and before he could perhaps wheedle something out of me I took my departure. Beryl was reading in the lounge when I got in. She glanced up at me.

'So they got the maniac,' she said.

'Yes, that's right. They — ' I broke off and stared at her. 'How did you know?'

'Inspector Hilton came to tell me this afternoon.'

'So that was why he was so evasive,' I breathed. 'Trying to get me separate from you and match up both lots of statements —'

Beryl asked slowly, 'You called on him, then? Just why?'

'Only to see how far he'd got with the Harkness murder.'

'Your concern over Harkness is most touching,' she commented dryly, tossing down her book. 'It would be more truthful to say that you really wanted to discover if I had had anything to do with it, wouldn't it? I have already warned you, Dick, not to dabble in things which do not concern you.'

'This does concern me!' I shouted.

'I think,' she said, 'you had better freshen up for dinner.'

The hot retort I had ready died. I left the room, tidied up and came down to dinner in silence. It was as I ate that my eye wandered to the book Beryl had been reading. It was Calcot's *Advanced Astronomy*.

'It happens to interest me,' Beryl remarked, following my gaze. 'In fact in these days it is about the only thing that does interest me. There is something rather wonderful . . . about space and time.'

'I suppose so,' I said. No use reminding her she had never even looked at a star in the old days, let alone studied astronomy. Then I got to thinking about the blood-stone. 'Perhaps from a passing meteor or outer space,' that write-up had said . . . Lord! I decided to look at that textbook more closely if I ever got the chance.

Dinner over and our conversation none too free we took up positions on opposite sides of the lounge. Beryl took up her textbook again and I scowled through the evening paper. First chance I had had so far to look through it, and pretty soon I came across something that hit me right between the eyes.

Ordinarily it would not have meant a thing, for it was only a tiny column, but now —

FAMOUS SOPRANO
FOUND MURDERED

I read the report hurriedly. It stated that Madame Elva Borini, famous Italian prima donna, had been found mysteriously murdered in her Naples villa that morning. Found by her maid. The famous singer had had a sash cord wrapped three times round her neck and knotted. Police were investigating, and so on and so on.

I looked up with a grim face over my newspaper. I was on the point of asking Beryl if she had ever heard of Madame Borini when her eyes lifted from her book and looked straight into mine — calmly, insolently. Completely and utterly the question went out of my mind. But the mystery of the business remained —

This was getting beyond all reason. A woman in Italy had died in precisely the same fashion as Boyd Harkness — But how? Definitely Beryl could not have done it, separated by a thousand miles of land and sea. Or could she . . . ?

I started thinking then about the other people I'd read about — the remaining owners of the bloodstone jewel sections. Suppose they too were marked down? That the jewel had something to do with it I was now quite convinced. Could I warn them somehow? No. That would draw the whole attention of the law to Beryl and me, and I considered the mystery about her was a matter for me alone to solve.

One thing I did know. I had got to see inside that cellar of hers. She had warned me to keep out, but just now things were so complex I had just got to act. I came to a decision.

Going upstairs, I got four sleeping tablets from the phial in the bathroom cupboard, and returned downstairs with them in my pocket. Beryl looked at me rather curiously, and on the incredible assumption that she could perhaps read thoughts I purposely diverted my mind from my intention. Back went her eyes to her textbook.

We had a light supper of biscuits and wine, during which process I took good care to slip the four tablets into her glass unnoticed. Then, without a word to each other we made tracks for retiring . . .

5

It worked! Inside thirty minutes Beryl was sleeping like a log; but I waited until the hall clock boomed out one before I moved, then I slipped into pants, shirt and shoes, sped downstairs and got my torch from the library desk.

I found the cellar door under the stairs tightly locked — and a new lock at that. Beryl had had the old one replaced with one of the most foolproof and expensive ones made.

Back I went upstairs, searched around for some sign of a key. At last I found it, on a silk cord round her neck. In fact there were two keys on the ring.

Gently I disentangled the cord and hurried back, found the appropriate key and swung the cellar door open gently.

I stepped forward, closed the door behind me, switched on my torch so that the beam fell down the stone steps. Queer, to pay rent for this darned place and I'd never been allowed to see the basements!

I hurried down to the first basement, went through its emptiness to the second one. What I beheld here was neither revolting nor terrible: all the dark thoughts I'd conjured up had been groundless. What I saw was more surprising than anything else.

There was quite a deal of electrical apparatus, with cables soldered very professionally to the main house power wire. This feed wire led back to a device that looked like a carbon arc holder. In fact that was exactly what it was, when I looked more closely — only it was of unusual design with a metal matrix fixed at the carbon point gaps, what for I had no idea.

In a far corner was something like a long cylinder, half completed, with little tubes sprouting out of one end. It looked very like a bomb. Its metal was enormously tough and burnished, as though intended to stand an enormous amount of wear and tear.

The rest comprised a bench full of up-to-date tools — all for metalwork apparently. There was also a chunk of wax among other things, which gave me the bright inspiration of taking an impression of the two keys I had got . . .

That seemed to be everything — No, not everything, for my final glance around revealed a shelf in the shadows on which reposed a number of new books. So far everything was checking up. Beryl had said books, instruments, and odds and ends . . . Right!

First book I took down was a new edition of *Gems, Stones, and their Origins*, identical with the library copy I had studied. I flipped the pages and studied the column about the bloodstone. Significant and obvious thing!

The names of the owners of the quartered bloodstone were underlined in red ink! Even more significant, the names of Boyd Harkness and Madame Elva Borini were ticked in red over the top. A sort of mute 'Account settled.'

I went hastily through the rest of the books. They were brand new up-to-date Directories most of them — one for London, one for Naples, Italy, a smaller one giving particulars of addresses of British officials in Bermuda — The address of Boyd Harkness had not been necessary anyway, being close at hand. But Lord! What! How? Of all the riddles I'd ever heard of, this took the biscuit — and I was right in the middle of it.

I came finally upon a notepad among

the books. On it, obviously culled from the reference books, were the full addresses of the four bloodstone jewel owners . . . but not only their addresses. Also given was the exact latitude and longitude where their homes were placed on the Earth's surface! That, and a maze of figuring, that made no sense whatever to me.

For a long time I puzzled over this new enigma, but nothing clicked in my mind. I was beaten — at the moment. I put the books and note-pad back, prepared to retreat, then I caught sight of a massive new safe in a corner near the entrance of the basement. The second key's use became immediately apparent.

Once I'd opened the safe door the first thing to hit the beam of my torch was a flood of ruby, bloodlike radiance.

Carefully I took out the heavy mass, studied its amazing lustrous depths in awe. Beyond doubt, Harkness' paper-weight, sent by mail to Beryl. But why should he send it to her when he didn't even know her? And why murder afterwards — ? But there, I was getting on the deep side again. I needed more obvious things right now.

The safe contained nothing else, so at last I put the stone back and went back to bed, put the keys safely back round Beryl's neck. She did not move in the least — and I had a wax lump in my coat pocket . . .

I slept badly, brooding — At last dawn crept to the windows.

* * *

If Beryl suspected anything of my nocturnal activities she showed no sign of it. As we breakfasted her manner was still that of cold aloofness. I went out again in the same brusque way, determined to spend my day doing a lot of hard thinking instead of going to my office. I was getting too wound up to think straight much longer . . .

I felt it was as inevitable as the sunrise that before long death would overtake the two remaining bloodstone owners — Carson of London and Cardew of Bermuda. But still I didn't see how I could stop it without getting across the track of the law, and that was the last thing I wanted. Nor could I get any truth out of Beryl: between us loomed that invisible, merciless wall.

I had driven the car out of the drive and on to the main village road, thinking deeply as I went, when I saw the postman approaching on an ancient bicycle. I hailed him.

'Anything for me?'

He got off his machine, wheeled it over and stuck a horny finger and thumb through his little bundle.

'No, I'm afraid not, Mr. Shaw. Not this — But I'm forgetting this parcel!' He dived in his bag and brought a smallish brown paper one to light.

'For Mrs. Shaw,' he said, then as he studied it, 'And air mail too. Foreign airmail. Rare round here. Must be important, Plenty of weight for air mail — '

'Be all right. I'll take it for her,' I said. 'No need to go all the way to the house with it.'

'Well. I — Okay, it'll be all right,' he

nodded, handing it over. 'Rare we get two parcels for the same place two days running. Things have livened up a bit in the parcel mail since you and your wife came, Mr. Shaw. That one the day before yesterday and this one to-day — '

'That's what mails are for, isn't it?' I interrupted him shortly. 'Thanks!'

I drove on again rather hurriedly, but for some reason I felt he was watching me go. He *was*: my rear mirror showed it. Irritated, I drove on until I was out of his sight, then stopped and examined the parcel hurriedly. Airmail express, stamped 'Napoli, Italia.'

I ripped off the cords, tore away the paper, opened a strong cardboard box —

Within a bed of cotton wool was a glowing chunk of red glasslike stone . . .

Thoughts just wouldn't come to me. I was stunned. One thousand miles away a total stranger had mailed Beryl a piece of an antique jewel. And airmail to be sure of top speed. Then — then Madame Borini had been murdered, same as Boyd Harkness . . . It gave me cold shudders to think of it. I began to get an insight upon the hellish, super-natural thing I was living with. More! Married to it!

And the law too showed signs that it might catch up. Inspector Hilton was nobody's fool. The postman was already a nosey kind of individual, and had noted the parcels arriving. If he told the police —

Something happened to me at this point in my thoughts. Don't ask me what it was because I can't tell you. I simply became aware that my skin was pricking and that the road and the car were both swaying unnaturally. It was like being on the edge of a faint — Only it wasn't a faint because I started the car up, reversed, and went back to the house.

I picked up the jewel in its box, let myself in by the front door and went right through to the lounge. Beryl was there, as though waiting for me. She was smiling imperturbably. I put the box down on the table beside her without a word, went out again, drove away again in my car . . .

The dreamlike sensation left me suddenly, left me limp and breathless. I was drawn up on the side of the road where I had stopped before. Had I been asleep, or what — Had I *really* been back home? I searched around the car frantically but the jewel and its box had gone as though it had never been.

What in thunder? Had it been a delusion . . . ?

'No,' I whispered, taking myself in hand. 'No, that was no delusion. Get it through your head that you've got to work on this before it's too late. You are not fighting just your wife but something diabolical that can do just as it likes with you — and her probably. You're dealing with the unknown — a vast, overpowering unknown!'

Yes, that was right! While I gathered my thoughts I drove on again slowly, towards the village. I was passing the local police headquarters when Hilton came suddenly into view in the doorway. He had evidently seen my approach through the window. He hailed me, came to the side of the car as I stopped.

'Glad you dropped past — save me the trouble of runnin' up to your place yet awhile, but I'll go up later anyway an' have a word or two with your wife . . . Just routine, you know.'

'Yes, of course,' I nodded, searching his face. Then casually, 'Something wrong? Something new, I mean?'

'In a way,' he said. 'Still the Harkness job, of course. The Yard are on to it now, but I'm still nosin' around a bit. Y'see, it seems one of Harkness' last acts was to send off a parcel. His servant mailed it — accordin' to later questionin' — and he says it was sent to your wife . . . ' Hilton rubbed his whiskery jaw. 'An' that's sort of queer,' he mused. 'She said she'd never seen Harkness when I asked her about him. Remember?'

'I remember,' I said shortly. 'And so far as I know it is true. Anyway, what has this to do with Harkness' death?'

'Never can tell . . . You say you never met Harkness neither?'

I shook my head impatiently. 'Of course not! And if he sent a parcel to my wife there was probably a very good reason for it. A — a neighbourly act, perhaps . . . '

'Oh, very neighbourly.' Hilton studied me impersonally for a moment, then he said, 'Even by itself it would be queer — no denyin' it: but when the postal authorities in the village tell us yet another parcel was received today for your wife, from Italy by airmail — a rare thing in these parts — it begins to look more 'n just queer. It's none of our business, of course, but we do know that an Italian singer died in the same way as Harkness. Seems odd that both folks died after sendin' parcels to your wife, doesn't it?'

'What the devil have events in Italy to do with you?' I blustered.

'Nothin',' he admitted blandly. 'But sometimes the police in different countries find things to help each other . . . Well, I'll keep you no longer, Mr. Shaw. Probably see you later when I call on your wife.'

He returned leisurely to his headquarters and I drove on again grimly, not caring where I went. So the postman had talked! I might have known it — The damned, driveling old fool! The police were on to the hunt now, and if they found those jewel pieces they'd probably arrest Beryl there and then. Somehow I had got to protect her. She was still my wife . . .

Somehow I formulated a plan out of the chaos. I drove on into the city, and had two keys made from my wax impression block. It took an hour, during which time I grabbed some lunch, then I set off back home. I arrived in the early afternoon, declutched the car into the garage to make no sound, then silently entered the house.

My idea was to perhaps surprise Beryl in some guilty act. But instead it was me that got the surprise. Beryl was in the lounge, lying on the divan fast asleep. At least I thought she was. Her book on astronomy lay on the floor beside her dangling hand, and she lay breathing softly with her eyes closed. I wondered if the dosage of sleeping tablets was having still a latent effect.

Softly I moved out into the hall again, and nearly collided with Mrs. Wilson.

'Mrs. Shaw been out at all today?' I asked her quickly.

'No, Mr. Shaw — not at all.'

'Anybody called? Inspector Hilton

— or the postman perhaps?'

'Why, no, Mr. Shaw.' Mrs. Wilson gave me a mystified look. 'Is anything wrong, sir? This morning you returned hurriedly with a small box, and now you are back long before your usual time. Can I get you something — ?'

'I *did* come back then, with a box?' I gripped her arm.

'Surely: I saw you from the hall here. You didn't look very well, I might add.'

'No — I didn't feel it. Did you see what happened to that box after I left it in the lounge?'

'As I recall, your wife went into the basement with it.' Mrs. Wilson nodded rather dubiously to the closed door under the staircase.

I thought a moment, then said, 'Okay, that's all. And you have not seen me this afternoon — remember that! It's in everybody's interests that you say that. I've an idea some trouble is blowing up.'

She nodded slowly and went off to the domestic regions. I returned to the lounge to make sure Beryl was still asleep. She was. Picking up her book I looked at the page she had been reading.

It was all about the stars in our galaxy — and the possibility of other planetary systems — a long and highly technical treatise concerning the possibility of life on those far distant worlds swirling in the Milky Way untold light years away.

Interesting? In a sense . . . and again I thought of that statement that the bloodstone might have come from outer space. Just for a second I hovered on the verge of the revolting, incredible truth — then I couldn't pursue it any further for Beryl stirred very slightly.

I made myself scarce immediately, hurried to the cellar, unlocked the door with my duplicate key and closed it behind me. Inside of five minutes I had hidden myself into the deepest shadows of the first cellar where I could watch and not be watched. I was in the dark, my heart thumping. I no longer had illusions about Beryl. If she discovered me she'd probably kill me . . .

After I had waited for about ten minutes the door opened at the top of the steps. Good! My hope that she might come down here was being realized . . . A switch clicked. Dim light illumined the cellar steps. She closed the door behind her, descended the steps quickly, walked right past the place where I was concealed and into the contiguous cellar. Another light came on. I watched intently.

Her face had lost something of the frozen calm she usually registered upon it: rather she was looking worried. No — something more than that, even. Distraught! Like somebody working at top speed against an emergency.

The first thing she did was to take down the writing-pad on which she had made some complicated notes about latitude and longitude. For a while she studied them, then nodded slowly, began to think out aloud in a tone I could just catch —

'If these mathematics are right and the wavelength of thought is correct, I cannot miss. It succeeded with the Italian woman and Harkness: no reason why it should not succeed with London and Bermuda. Yes — it must be right. It has got to be right!' she finished

She became quiet and left me puzzling. Wavelength of *thought*? What in blue blazes did she mean? Then I watched again. She went to the safe and took out two chunks of red jewel — Harkness' and the one I'd brought back in the morning obviously — and laid them on her bench.

She tested the facets carefully, finally found two that matched exactly. These she bound together with a spring-clip device and then put them in the matrix of her carbon-arc frame. Donning dark glasses she switched on the power and I had to jerk my eyes away from that searing white core of flame as she went to work.

At the end of it, through a haze of pink spots, I saw that the two jewels had merged into one. As Beryl turned it about in her fingers it looked like the half of an immense diamond — and exact diamond-shape too. But the half-way line was rough and broken, obviously needing two more pieces to finish it.

That brought a chill of horror back into my mind. Only Carson of London, and Cardew of Bermuda could supply those pieces. Were they *already* — ? Was that what Beryl had been doing, by some mystic process, when she had apparently been asleep? Lord!

Evidently satisfied she put the fused jewel back into the safe, slammed the door, then turned to the queer cylinder thing I had noted the previous night. Carefully, with the air of an expert technician, she went to work on it. She got busy with an electric welder, a hacksaw, a metal cutting lathe — Yes, she even fitted something that was darned close to an armature. Of course this was all crazy, for before the car accident she had not even known the ignition from the carburettor on an automobile. Yet *now* . . .

The more she handled that object the more I began to guess at what it really was. It was some kind of rocket. The shining belly was there, the tubes for rocket firing — *Other planets*! The two things sort of added up all at once to mean something, but I still did not know what.

Then Beryl looked up sharply. For an instant I thought she had become aware

183

of my presence; then I realized there was a sharp knocking on the cellar door and the voice of Mrs. Wilson. Beryl looked annoyed, put down her tools, then went up the stairs and switched off the lights as she went.

I caught Mrs. Wilson's words, 'There's the Inspector here again, madam — ' Then the door had closed.

6

Inspector Hilton! Things were blowing up for a showdown and no mistake. I waited a moment or two until I heard Beryl's footsteps move away from the hall, followed by Hilton's heavier tread. They'd gone into the lounge.

I crept up the cellar steps, let myself out into the hall and closed the door again softly. Silently I moved across the hall, paused outside the door of the lounge and listened. Hilton was speaking.

' — and so naturally, Mrs. Shaw, I felt it necessary to ask you a question or two. Why should Mr. Harkness, a complete stranger to you, send you a parcel?'

'You have taken rather a lot for granted, Inspector,' Beryl's cold voice retorted. 'When I said neither my husband nor I had ever seen Harkness I did not mean he was a stranger. I have corresponded with him, even telephoned him, many a time. But we never met.'

Lies! Absolute lies!

'No letters were found from you, Mrs. Shaw,' Hilton observed. Then after an ominous pause, 'And what was the nature of this — er — elusive acquaintance?'

'Antiques, if you must know. If you were anything of an antique collector yourself you would know there are no lengths to which ardent collectors will not go to further their hobbies. I corresponded with Harkness over antiques. He promised to send me a very interesting specimen from his collection — and he did so. That it happened to be on the day of his death was pure coincidence.'

'An' what did he send you?'

'A piece of heavy coloured glass.'

'The paperweight, eh? Just as I thought. An' why didn't you mention it when I said a paperweight had disappeared?'

'How was I to know the paperweight and jewel were related?' Beryl asked sternly. 'You'd be well advised, Inspector, to gather a little more evidence directly concerned with Harkness' murder before you start piling up absurd data. I'm answering no more questions! Not until you've a definite reason for questioning me, anyway. You can consider yourself lucky I've obliged you so far . . . Now, I have work to do — '

'I suppose,' Hilton's unabashed voice interrupted, 'you were interested enough in antiques to also correspond with a Madame Borini, in Italy?'

'Yes, I was,' Beryl admitted after a pause. 'She sent me an antique only this morning as a matter of fact.'

'Uh-huh,' Hilton acknowledged pensively, then in a sharp voice, 'Ever hear of a jewel called — the bloodstone?'

'Ever hear of confining yourself to facts?' Beryl snapped. 'I've told you already I've had enough of this cross-examination! From your tone one would imagine you're accusing me of murdering

Boyd Harkness, and then a woman in far away Italy just after they sent me their bloodstone jewels — '

'So that is what they did send?' Hilton's voice asked softly, as Beryl stopped dead. 'Thanks, Mrs. Shaw. Thanks very much . . . '

There were footsteps. I'd only just time to dodge when Hilton came hurrying out. Quick as a flash I bolted for the hall's rear window, scrambled through it and dropped into the grounds. For an hour after that I cooled my heels in the garage, then at the normal time for coming home I came in the front door as usual and walked into the lounge.

Beryl looked at me sharply and I was forced to drop my gaze under the piercing stare of her blue eyes. That look was back — the look that went through me, through the room, through the wall — Somewhere. *To another planet?* What a speculation that was!

'You're back a little early, Dick,' Beryl said, and my astounding meditation snapped right off.

'Er — yes. Not much doing today. How about you?'

She did not answer at all. Her eyes were still watching me. I felt, I *knew* she suspected me of something, and was trying with every fiendish device at her command to squeeze it out of me. But I baulked her by giving my mind no chance to dwell on what I knew. For by now I was sure she could read thoughts plainly . . .

This sort of thing kept up until dinner was on the table, then as she ate she asked an abrupt question.

'Do you happen to know Inspector Hilton's Christian name?'

I stared in astonishment. 'Why, no. What on earth does it matter?'

'It matters more than you will ever perhaps realize.' Then with that problematical reply I saw that distraught look come back briefly to her face. Suddenly she mastered it, aware of my gaze, and went on eating. Nor did she make any further reference to her baffling request . . .

The moment the meal was over she switched on the television and sat watching intently to the news bulletin. I listened too, not much interested — until towards the end.

'*A curious form of murder by strangulation seems to have become an international mystery lately,*' the announcer said. '*First Boyd Harkness, the famous candy king, died that way: then Madame Elva Borini of Italy suffered the same fate yesterday. Today comes news of two more inexplicable murders — that of Henry Carson of London, a well-known sportsman, and Doctor Kenneth Cardew, an attaché to the British Embassy in Bermuda. Both men were found murdered in identical fashion, with cord wrapped three times round the neck and then knotted. The strange similarity of the cases is causing the police of the countries concerned to suspect an international gang . . .*'

Beryl switched off sharply and sat gazing into space. The only sign of emotion she showed was a slight twitching of her fingers. And me? Well, I wasn't stunned because I had known it was coming. But what did get me was how it had been done. That reference to 'thought wavelength' she had made in the cellar kept recurring to me too. So much so I

189

presently posed what was apparently an idle question.

'Berry, I've often wondered if it is possible to kill people by thought. Ever consider that?'

I don't know why I asked the question: just that I was fed up and wanted to find her Achilles Heel. And it looked as though I'd managed it for every trace of color drained out of her cheeks and left her eyes burning at me like sunken holes.

'Why do you want to know?' Her voice was like steel wire under sudden strain.

I plunged. 'Because you killed four people and there was no way to do it except by *thought*!' I shouted. 'Do you take me for a fool, Berry? I don't know how you do it — but I do know you have *done* it! You've had these people send you their four parts of their bloodstone, one of which I intercepted this morning. The others will be here! I know that! This morning you hypnotized me over a distance: and you have done it before. Now the police are on it, and they'll get you. In God's name, Berry, what are you trying to do?' I finished desperately. 'I'm your husband aren't I? Tell me!'

'You fool,' she whispered, crouched back in her chair. 'You contemptible, pitiable fool!'

Then she jerked suddenly to her feet and swept out of the room, and went hurrying upstairs. I was left to brood, piecing together the fragments of what I knew already. I got nowhere, so at last I went to bed.

I looked in on her and found Beryl asleep as though nothing in the world were different. But for me one thought was dinning through my brain: why had she wanted the Christian name of Inspector Hilton . . . ?

Next morning, immediately after breakfast, things happened. I was about to leave the house as usual when the postman arrived and rang noisily.

He handed in two parcels to me — for I'd waved Mrs. Wilson away, being already at the door myself — and I had just time to see they were airmail and express delivery and stamped Bermuda and London respectively, when the door was pushed firmly aside and Inspector

Hilton came in. With him was a police inspector and two plain clothes men.

'Mornin' Mr. Shaw,' Hilton said.

I nodded unthinkingly to the breakfast room and he strode ahead of me. I'll not easily forget the way Beryl looked up from the table when she saw the Inspector, the officials, and me holding two boxes. She looked as though dead for a moment, then with a supreme effort she mastered herself and stood up.

'I'm Detective Inspector Peterson, New Scotland Yard,' said the inspector briefly, then glancing at the parcels, 'we've been waiting to see if these came along. You will open them, please, in my presence. Here's my authority . . . ' He tossed down a form on the table.

Beryl obeyed slowly as I put the parcels down. From each one she took a red jewel.

'Complete,' she whispered, half to herself. '*Complete*!'

'Final pieces of the bloodstone,' Hilton snapped. 'And at the expense of the lives of the owners immediately afterwards — '

'By a method only you can know

about,' Peterson said curtly. 'I have a warrant here for your arrest, Mrs. Shaw — for murder!'

He held it out, granite-faced, but Beryl snatched it and threw it on the table, stared at us with blazing eyes.

'You idiot!' she screamed, glaring at Peterson so fiendishly he fell back a pace. 'Consummate idiot! What do I care for your silly warrants and authorities when I have a chosen task to perform? What do I — ?' She stopped, calmed again. 'Come with me, all of you,' she commanded. 'You want an explanation it seems: you shall have it!'

She led the way into the cellar depths and switched on the lights. Hilton, Peterson, and the others looked around them in wonder, then waited in grim silence while she brought forth the remainder of the fused jewel. The cellar flashed with cream radiances while she fused the final pieces, left all of us dazzled. At the end of it Beryl had in her hand the most perfect diamond-shaped gem I had ever seen.

'You don't know what it is?' she asked

slowly, even contemptuously. 'Your dull earthbound minds regard it as a heavy piece of coloured glass, eh?'

'Experts say it has no value anyway,' Hilton retorted.

'Experts!' Beryl sneered. 'What do they know about it? This is nothing more or less than the Life Stone of Andura. Useless in separate pieces, but in its complete form capable of giving life eternal to a race infinitely different from Earth people. Under the influence of the cosmic radiations forever pouring on Andura this Life Stone gives out vital emanations, as vital to the people of Andura as the sun's rays are to the people of the Earth . . . '

We looked at each other. I was beginning to think I had guessed the truth.

'Where in thunder is Andura?' Peterson demanded, mystified.

'It is a planet, eleven light years distant, circling the star your astronomers call Procyon!'

My guess had been right then! But before any of us could comment Beryl turned away and put the jewel in a special matrix inside the little rocket cylinder she had made. She set some automatic gadget, then carried the thing through the outer door of the basement and into the grounds. Here we waited until the gadget worked. It fired an explosive and the rocket whipped skywards with amazing speed and was gone.

'Now,' Beryl whispered, eyes skywards, 'it doesn't matter what you do. My work is done. Small though it is, constructed using Anduran science that rocket will have enough power to drive beyond Earth's gravity field, then — once it is in free space and so accessible to the forces we use — it will be drawn inter-dimensionally through space by the scientists at work on Andura . . . On, on, on through the void, carrying life and new hope.'

'Look here, just what the hell is this?' Peterson demanded angrily. 'We came here to — '

'You shall have your explanation,' Beryl said quietly. 'Come back into the cellar . . . ' Then as we filed in,

'A strange tale perhaps. Ages ago that

Life Stone was stolen from Andura by an enemy. Forced to flee with it he dropped it in his space travels upon the Earth, in what later became Arkansas. He was never heard of again. But that Life Stone was needed if the Andurians were ever to regain their former glory of almost endless life. It had to be recovered. It was known to be on Earth, but physical differences made a journey to Earth outside the realm of safety for the Andurians. So, it demanded a go-between. We of Andura are masters of thought projection, which is not subject to material laws governing the speed of light. We decided to use an inhabitant of this world as a servant. This body was chosen, its real will and individuality suppressed while my own thought projection took over . . . '

The bewildering explanation and change in tenses brought a cry from me.

'But Berry, what are you saying? You're not an Andurian: you are Beryl Shaw, my wife!'

'I have her body,' she said gravely, and you've no idea how odd the statement sounded. 'I transferred my mind to hers,

196

and the sudden consequence of that caused a motor accident. It could have been any body — but hers happened to be the one. So, this body doesn't matter to me. It can't hurt me if it gets hurt — hence injuries and knife cuts which so amazed you . . . '

She smiled cynically as I recalled that peculiar mystery.

'My job was to search for the Life Stone, using this earth woman's body for the purpose,' she went on. 'I found it, partly by mind reading and partly from studying books. I found out it was called a bloodstone and was split in four. In the hospital I had time to read minds, orient myself, and learn the language . . . '

Now things were fitting in. Her queer amnesia, her lack of knowledge concerning trivial things — Of course!

'Thought,' she said, 'is a supreme weapon! If you are the master of it you can do anything, even hurl your mind across infinity as I have done. Even you on Earth know that the brain sends out tiny electrical impulses: these impulses can be directed or received as easily as you control radio. Hypnotism and psychology are commonplace to you. But actual thought waves have a special ultra short length and can be directed anywhere, instantaneously. All I had to do therefore was to determine the exact position on the Earth's surface of the people I wanted, send forth a hypnotic command for them to forward me their bloodstone: and then issue a second command for them to kill themselves. This I did in case they afterwards came to question why they had sent their bloodstone jewel away, and sought to recover it. Otherwise I would have spared them: I have no real wish to kill. I did it for safety, and I chose strangling by rope for simplicity, because I am not fully acquainted with the mechanisms of your revolvers . . .

'As mischance had it, one of the people I wanted — Harkness — lived quite near to here. That started the police off and made my work far more hurried than I had intended. I chose this lonely house so I could work in peace and quiet . . . And you fools talk of murder!'

'It's still murder!' Peterson shouted.

'You are Mrs. Shaw, and this is the biggest trick set-up I ever — '

Beryl looked at me. 'I could have killed you long ago,' she said slowly, 'but as I read your pathetic thoughts I felt sorry for you — sorry I had had to take your wife from you. Now I do not need to kill you because my job is done. But I see you still need proof . . . '

She looked at Hilton thoughtfully, then said, 'Usually I need the Christian name of a person to call them at a distance through hypnotic command. There are thousands of similar surnames, but few with the same Christian and surname. It makes the task easier — and had I known your Christian name before this, Hilton, you would not be here now. Now I do not need it because you stand here face to face . . . '

'Now wait a minute — ' he began, then he stopped with the words frozen on his lips, his eyes staring into hers fixedly.

I too — all of us — was held by that awful hypnotic grip as for the first time the inhuman intellectual power operating through Beryl flooded forth in all its power. Her eyes were deep pools of compulsion — iron, ruthless compulsion. Hilton turned slowly and took up a length of cord from the bench, began to wrap it three times round his neck.

He knotted it, started to draw it tightly. I screamed suddenly.

'Beryl! *Beryl!*'

The light died in her eyes. She looked almost wistful.

'Fools,' she sighed. 'Poor earthbound fools. Why should I kill this blundering ignoramus when I have shown you already what I can do? Usually I close my eyes and concentrate, then I — But what can you hope to know of thought projection over the wastes of space?'

She was silent for a moment, then staggered a little. I caught her quickly.

'Dick,' she whispered. 'Dick, what happened? Did the car blow up, run into something, or what — ?'

She looked up sharply, and her blue eyes were the same as I had always known them to be — clear, vital, alive.

'Where — where on earth are we?' she gasped.

'Procyon,' Hilton whispered, sweating as he took the cord off his neck. '*Gone! Back to Procyon* — '

'And try making that murder charge stick now,' I said to Peterson, as his jaw lolled stupidly. 'You can't do it — '

'Is — is this your wife or not?' he breathed, staring at the mystified Beryl.

'*This*,' I said slowly, 'is my wife. The other was only her body.'

'What other?' Beryl demanded. 'What monkey business is going on here?'

'Upstairs,' I said briefly, taking her arm. 'We all need a drink. Then there's a tale to tell . . . '

THE END

CLIMATE INCORPORATED
THE FIVE MATCHBOXES
EXCEPT FOR ONE THING
BLACK MARIA, M.A.
ONE STEP TOO FAR
THE THIRTY-FIRST OF JUNE
THE FROZEN LIMIT
ONE REMAINED SEATED
THE MURDERED SCHOOLGIRL
SECRET OF THE RING
OTHER EYES WATCHING
I SPY . . .
FOOL'S PARADISE
DON'T TOUCH ME
THE FOURTH DOOR
THE SPIKED BOY
THE SLITHERERS
MAN OF TWO WORLDS
THE ATLANTIC TUNNEL
THE EMPTY COFFINS
LIQUID DEATH
PATTERN OF MURDER
NEBULA
THE LIE DESTROYER
PRISONER OF TIME

MIRACLE MAN
THE MULTI-MAN
THE RED INSECTS
THE GOLD OF AKADA
RETURN TO AKADA
GLIMPSE
ENDLESS DAY
THE G-BOMB
A THING OF THE PAST
THE BLACK TERROR
THE SILENT WORLD
DEATH ASKS THE QUESTION
A CASE FOR BRUTUS LLOYD
LONELY ROAD MURDER
THE HAUNTED GALLERY
SPIDER MORGAN'S SECRET
BURY THE HATCHET

We do hope that you have enjoyed reading this large print book.

Did you know that all of our titles are available for purchase?

We publish a wide range of high quality large print books including:
Romances, Mysteries, Classics
General Fiction
Non Fiction and Westerns

Special interest titles available in large print are:
The Little Oxford Dictionary
Music Book, Song Book
Hymn Book, Service Book

Also available from us courtesy of Oxford University Press:
Young Readers' Dictionary
(large print edition)
Young Readers' Thesaurus
(large print edition)

For further information or a free brochure, please contact us at:
Ulverscroft Large Print Books Ltd.,
The Green, Bradgate Road, Anstey,
Leicester, LE7 7FU, England.
Tel: (00 44) **0116 236 4325**
Fax: (00 44) **0116 234 0205**

DEPARTMENT OF SPOOKS

Ernest Dudley

A high-level diplomat, about to assume a vital posting at the United Nations, is being blackmailed. But if he goes to the police and prosecutes, his career will be finished. Even though the press can only report him as Mr. X, his well-known face will be clearly revealed to everyone in court. So Government special agent Mike Hammond is given his orders: 'Winkle this blackmailer out, and he's all yours. You're judge, jury and — and executioner.'

THE HEEL OF ACHILLES

Gerald Verner

'*I'm done for . . . find X.1 . . . Dene . . . You must . . . Tooth-paste . . .* ' England is at war with Germany and Dene of the Secret Service tries to decipher his fatally wounded colleague's garbled message — potentially vital information for England's survival. Who is X.1? What does the word *Tooth-paste* signify? Dene must find out and stop X.1, or the Third Reich will strike a crippling blow to England and change the course of the war. And he has just eight days in which to do it . . .

DEAD SECRET

Gerald Verner

Criminologist Felix Heron and his wife, Thelma, investigate Sir Percival Trench's death on the hunting field. The inquest's verdict is that it was an accident, but his fiancée thinks otherwise. The case becomes increasingly complex, not least when it appears that Sir Percival's fortune of two hundred and twenty thousand pounds has vanished. Then, when the dead body of a 'grass' is found hanging on a tree — Heron has plenty to work on before finding an unexpected solution.

THE POISON CUPBOARD

J. F. Burke

Hardworking Laura Swanton, a local G.P., has lavished all her affection on her wastrel twin brother. But then he is sent to prison and his wife — of whose existence Laura has been unaware — comes to live with her and her mother. Laura's initial contempt for this woman curdles into vicious dislike, which finally becomes an obsession. Somehow she must avert this threat to the very foundation of her existence. Somehow — but how?

MARKED FOR MURDER

Norman Lazenby

'Leave this affair alone, Martinson
— Jean Hallison is dead . . . ' The
caller had rung off, leaving Inspector
Jim Martinson wondering if this was
a bluff. Had Jean been murdered?
And where did the suave, grinning
Montoni fit in? He was accused of
assaulting two women — but at the
same time Jim himself had been
watching him elsewhere. Now, however, Jim links the chain of evidence
— slowly tightening the rope that will
bring in the sinister gang that is
terrorising Framcastle.